THE BOOK OF
HAVANA

EDITED BY ORSOLA CASAGRANDE

Translated by Orsola Casagrande
and Séamas Carraher

With special thanks to
Felix Julio Alfonso Lopez and J. M. Arrugaeta

First published in Great Britain in 2018 by Comma Press
commapress.co.uk

'Love in the Big City' ('Amor de ciudad grande') by Eduardo Heras León was first published in the collection *La Dolce Vita* (Ediciones Unión, 2012). A version of 'And all Because of that Fucking Spanish Kid' ('Por culpa de un jodido bicho español') by Daniel Chavarria was first published in the collection *El aguacate y la virtud* (Ediciones Matanzas, 2011). An 'Ali Khan Day' ('Un día de Alí Khan') by Francisco López Sacha was first published in the collection *Variaciones del arte de la fuga* (Ediciones Unión, 2011). 'Diary of a Serial Killer in the Jurassic' ('Diario de un asesino del Jurásico') by Jorge Enrique Lage was first published in the collection *El color de la sangre diluida* (Editorial Letras Cubanas, 2008). 'The List' ('Inventario') by Ahmel Echevarría Perè was first published in the collection *Inventario* (Ediciones Unión, 2004).

A CIP catalogue record of this book is available from the British Library.

ISBN: 1910974013
ISBN-13: 978-1910974018

The publisher gratefully acknowledges assistance from Arts Council England.

Printed and bound in England by Clays.

Contents

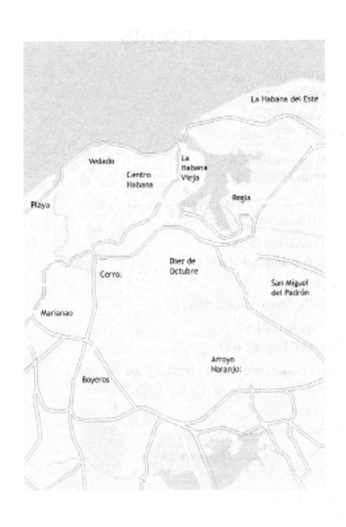

Introduction

HAVANA WASN'T ALWAYS WHERE it is today. The Villa of San Cristobal de La Habana had, in fact, two different locations before 16 November 1516, when it finally settled in its present location: a level stretch of land around a beautiful, wide bay, facing gentle hills to the south, and, to the east, the elevated embankment that became the site of the famous fortress 'La Cabaña'. Havana was the fifth of the seven 'villas' established by the Castilian conquerors in the early sixteenth century. But for decades, it was little more than a remote settlement, constantly under threat of attack by pirates and corsairs, who invaded and ransacked it as they pleased, among them the French pirate Jacques de Sores.[1]

This early Havana was of little interest to the Spanish crown. Logistically it served merely as a base for the 'discovery', conquest and subsequent colonisation of the Americas, both north and south. After acknowledging the importance and wealth of its newly conquered lands, the Spanish monarchy gradually became aware of the strategic geographic importance of Havana and its bay. Thus, from the mid-sixteenth to the late-eighteenth century, the city became the permanent headquarters of the so-called 'Spanish Treasure Fleet', a system of convoys linking Spain with its colonies across the Atlantic. This resulted in the city being fortified as well as having both war and merchant ships stationed in its harbour several months of the year. The fleet evolved into a huge convoy that, twice a year, set sail to Seville with the enormous wealth gained from its colonial looting; wealth which would be squandered subsequently in endless European wars.

INTRODUCTION

On 6 June, 1762, after a month of fierce resistance, the Villa of San Cristobal de La Habana fell to the forces of the British Empire. The 14,000 or so British soldiers, sailors and officers flooding into Havana that day would have found a city of just over 80,000 inhabitants, mostly residing in what, today, is Habana Vieja (Old Havana), as well as a few villages such as Gauanabacoa (now one of fifteen boroughs or precincts of modern Havana). We can only imagine today how the city must have appeared to these soldiers: a fiercely fortified port, a spectacular, sandy bay, and a bustling town constrained on its landward side by high city walls, still unfinished.

From that day in 1762, Havana and, with it, the western half of the island of Cuba, was, for eleven months only, 'British'; a brief but significant time during which the British allowed free trade and the large-scale introduction of African slaves. This lay the foundations for a prosperity rooted in the extension of slavery as a form of cheap, necessary labour for the expanding production of sugar and its derivatives – a 'bitter crop' that became the flagship product for the Cuban economy throughout the nineteenth century, along with other products, such as coffee and tobacco, that also played their part in the socio-cultural configuration of the emergent Cuban society.

After just eleven months, Havana and the other British-ruled parts of the island were returned to Spain in exchange for what is now Florida. But the physical evidence of this briefly 'British' Havana can still be explored today, even though, after the withdrawal of these temporary occupants, the elevated land around the city was fortified with three impressive fortresses: La Cabaña, the Castillo de Atarés (at the foot of the bay), and the Castillo del Príncipe (in the borough of Vedado). These still stand, in almost pristine condition, and probably represent the most complete and complex system of colonial fortifications in all of the Americas. The subsequent demolition of some of the city walls also allowed the necessary expansion of the city to the west, and to some extent to the south, giving way to the development and occupation of previously uninhabited flatlands – an urban development that is still ongoing.

Despite Havana's turbulent history, and economic and political importance, it isn't until the second decade of the nineteenth century that the city starts to appear in literature.[2]

In 1825, Alejandro de Humboldt published, in French, his *Political Essay on the Island of Cuba*, which can be considered a snapshot of the political economy of the country. This short and extraordinary book, widely rejected by the Cuban bourgeoisie for its scathing criticism of slavery, opened the way for a literary style that spread throughout the nineteenth century: a species of documentary travelogue, fascinated with Cuba, that almost became a genre of its own. These were usually written to a high literary standard and distinguished by detailed, insightful observation. It is a style in which research, description and personal impression predominate, dictated, of course, by the parameters of contemporary European sensibilities.

The best known work in this genre is undoubtedly *Journey to Havana* by Maria de Las Mercedes Santa Cruz y Montalvo, the Countess of Merlin. The author belonged to a wealthy middle-class family of Cuban slave owners, and had lived in Spain since her teens before relocating to Paris, where she kept up a busy social and cultural life. Curiously, Spanish language readers never had the opportunity to read the original version of this book – written in French and published in three separate volumes simply as *Havana* (Paris, 1844). Interestingly, this version of the book was both much longer and far more critical of the colonial realities of Cuban society than the self-censored version she later allowed to be published in Spanish, and circulated in Cuba.

This female-dominated travel literature, despite being over a century and a half old, is still interesting to read thanks to its accessibility, being written in a vibrant, highly descriptive prose style that conveys a vivid sense of the city at the time. Not just a vivid sense of the people living in Havana during this period, but also of many buildings, streets and squares that still stand exactly as they were. Also, despite being considered 'light' literature, these texts were not without social criticism of their time: reflecting a city undergoing a significant period of transition, with the ending of slavery, and the first whisperings of an independence movement, that is to say the growing Cuban aspiration towards self-rule.

Alongside these travel journals, a clearly identifiable literature began to emerge: an act of self-conscious creation more concerned with defining a 'national' narrative than being part of colonial ones.

Nineteenth-century Cuban literature reflects, in different ways, the social and political customs and contradictions of a nation-state gradually taking shape and finding its voice. Obviously in this process of literary creation, the capital, the largest city, has a special place. The literary output of this period is abundant and diverse, spanning all genres, although one text – generally regarded as *the* novel of nineteenth-century Havana – deserves special mention: *Cecilia Valdés* – a *costumbrismo* of the era, written and rewritten several times by its author, Cirilo Villaverde, before seeing a final version published in New York in 1882. This polyphonic narrative goes far beyond its plot (which revolves round various characters' rival and unsustainable affections for the beautiful mulatta, Cecilia), to transform itself into a detailed portrait inviting us to wander down from La Loma del Angel (Angel Hill), and through the streets of colonial Havana in the year 1830, a city full to the brim with racial, social and political contradictions.

From *Cecilia Valdés* onwards, the presence of the city in Cuban literature becomes almost inevitable. Moving forward into the twentieth century, Alejo Carpentier (1904-1980) reconstructed the city through carefully crafted Baroque works, set in disparate eras, ranging from the seventeenth century to the mid-twentieth. Entire chapters in *Baroque Concert, Explosion in a Cathedral,* and *Harassment* or the *Rite of Spring* are dominated by descriptions of the city. The pre-Castro Havana plays a similar, central role in the works of Guillermo Cabrera Infante (1929-2005), in particular his novel *Tres Tristes Tigres* (1966), and José Lezama Lima (1910-1976), most notably in his enigmatic, hermetic, semi-autobiographical, *Paradiso* (1966). We even discover the humble and often marginalised south side of the city in the Mario Conde detective series of Leonardo Padura Fuentes. It was not just novels that were inspired by the city; poetry, short fiction, drama, essay, music, film and the visual arts have all drawn immeasurably from the creative possibilities and personality of this urban space.

Two and a half million people bring life to this metropolis each day. In fact, almost continually since the 1920s, some 25% of the entire Cuban population has lived in the capital, making it not only a microcosm of Cuba, from the visiting world's point of view, but also a window for Cubans onto the rest of the world, and one that bears witness to its ever-fluctuating internal and external migration of people – increasingly an integral aspect of the Cuban experience.

If Havana effectively becomes a character all of its own for many of Cuba's twentieth century storytellers and poets, we should note that Cuban authors in more recent decades have tended to look at it in a different way, and occasionally, to *not* look at it at all, even taking it for granted, letting it fade into the background or backdrop of its characters' lives and suffering, a common stage, and one that doesn't hold the charm that it once did. This is certainly the case in several of the stories here. The reason is simple: the Havana they speak of encompasses as many sins as it does virtues.

The revolutionary triumph of 1959 halted the international

real estate speculation that had begun in that decade, and therefore kept intact to some extent Havana's original architectural fabric, effectively freezing it into a living museum for tourists keen to do some 'urban time travelling'. At the same time, the city has also suffered very real urban decay in its outer boroughs; areas which have seen exponential population growth met by largely low-quality social housing, and an increased sense of alienation from the 'centre' among its inhabitants. As these marginalised communities have grown, the problems and deficiencies in housing, transportation and basic services have increased.

This was compounded by the so-called 'Special Period' (*Período especial*), the intense period of economic crisis that followed the collapse of the Soviet Union. During this period (1989-mid-nineties), Cuba lost approximately 80% of its imports, and 80% of its exports; its GDP dropped by 34% and food and medicine imports stopped or severely slowed (on average, Cubans lost between 5% and 25% of their body weight), and nearly all of the country's petroleum imports from the USSR also stopped (Cuba's oil imports dropped to 10% of pre-1990 amounts).

The *bloqueo* – the US embargo in place since 1960 – complicated things even further during the Special Period, precisely because Cuba could not import what it needed (previously provided by the Soviet Union) from the US. Many outside Cuba saw its fate as a waiting game: only when the Castro dynasty came to an end would Cuba see real change. Now that this has finally happened (with Raúl handing over the presidency to Miguel Díaz-Canel just as we were going to press), Cubans themselves may still be proven right: life, for them, will only improve when attitudes outside the country change towards it. A glimmer of hope in this regard appeared four years ago, when normal diplomatic relations between the US and Cuba promised to be reestablished, following a joint communiqué from Presidents Raúl Castro and Barack Obama. But with the arrival of Trump, this hope was dashed as quickly as it had appeared.

Both the Special Period and these recent disappointments have had severe impacts on the city, not only further deteriorating its infrastructure but also deeply damaging the morale and psychology of its people: arousing both the desire to leave Cuba altogether, but also turning Havana into a magnet for internal migration and urbanisation, the city's tourism being one of the few industries that wasn't affected.

This combined physical, emotional and psychological deterioration perhaps sits at the heart of all the stories gathered here. Only one of the stories takes place before the Special Period: Eduardo del Llano's 'Into Tiny Pieces'. Set in the sprawling warren of prefabricated Soviet-style housing that makes up the Alamar district, this story takes us back to the mid-1970s with all its ideological zeal and extreme patriotism. The other nine stories deal directly, or indirectly, with the effects of the Special Period: its impact on the characters' lives, driving people towards violence or corruption, and colouring their aspirations (and desperation).

One of the indirect consequences of the Special Period was the 'centralising' of the city around its waterfront area. Havana placed more and more of its identity on these central locations overlooking the sea (Miramar, Vedado, Centro Habana, Habana Vieja), and other spots vital to tourism, while the rest of city became increasingly invisible.

What follows is a (by no means comprehensive) cross-section of Havana's very lively short story scene displaying – through different styles, sensibilities, approaches and ages – a fairly contemporary vision of Havana. A textual kaleidoscope of different sensitivies, and multiple observation points, hinting at the many layers and complexities developed by Cuban society over the last 30 years: a city made up of difficult if not impossible relationships, tragedies, struggles, despair and, yes, still some hope.

As the biographical notes will show, the authors here belong to different generations. Some of the 'less young' ones – Daniel Chavarria, Eduardo Heras León, Francisco López Sacha – already have well-established and deserved literary reputations. Others such as Eduardo del Llano, Amhel Echevarria, Laidi Fernández and Jorge Lage, although less well-known outside of Cuba, have major publications under their belts. Two authors – Irina J. Davidenko and R. Paredes – are actresses by profession, venturing from the world of the theatre directly into the world of the short story. While the youngest author here, Eduardo Angel Santiesteban, presents a fresh, contemporaneous story which offers a glimpse of where future generations may take the Cuban narrative. Literary styles are as diverse as their authors, of course, and all the techniques and storytelling tactics displayed here have antecedents in Cuba's rich and diverse literary traditions: semi-autobiographical realism, costumbrism, fantasy, irony and so forth. In this sense, they preserve, as well as give voice to, both the differences and the points of convergence of a literary tradition that, despite its apparently short history, has a wealth of depth and experience to draw on.

Orsola Casagrande
Havana, April 2018

Notes

1. Jacques de Sores, nicknamed 'The Exterminating Angel', was a French pirate who attacked and burnt Havana in 1555. Other than his attack on Havana, little is known of de Sores; he was the leader of a band of Huguenot pirates and a lieutenant or former lieutenant of another French pirate, François le Clerc, who was called 'Pegleg' or 'Jambe de Bois' on account of his wooden leg.

2. If we were to include the essay form, and the works of Cuban's 'first historians' (José Martin Félix de Arrate, Antonio José Valdés, Ignacio José Urrutia y Montoya, and others) this date should be set earlier, in the last decades of the eighteenth century.

Into Tiny Pieces[1]

Eduardo del Llano

'THE FLAG HAS FADED,' Áspera said one morning in 1977. 'What must the neighbours think? We'll have to buy a new one.'

Áspera's husband was a Party member, a lieutenant in the Reserves and a history lecturer at the technical college in Guira de Melena. Of course, his wife would never describe him in these terms. For her, he was someone who was forever dropping things or sitting on them, breaking them. Put him in an empty cave, and within minutes it would be in a mess.

The couple owned a large flag that they hung out on special days. These included not only national holidays and days of universal significance, but also days that were special to friends of theirs, birthdays, paydays, even the days when chicken arrived in the local state shop. The husband had a calendar with all these occasions marked on it: their wedding anniversary, for example, fell on the same day as Uganda's Independence Day. In the beginning, the flag only came out in mourning (on the anniversary of Martí's death,[2] for example) or on dates that only held a meaning for the enemy (4th July). But as time passed, they started hanging it out on other, happier occasions too; after all, you have to stand with the motherland in good times as well as bad. Because of this, but also because there was an unsightly damp spot on that stretch of wall which otherwise would have been seen from the street, it was no surprise prolonged exposure to bad weather had caused the national colours to fade.

1

And yes, it was faded. The red had been reduced to an anaemic brown around the star, and purple where it came in contact with the blue. The white parts were more like the colour you'd get from rinsing out paintbrushes in a kids nursery after a busy week of watercolours. It looked more like the flag of a Pacific atoll that had proclaimed sovereignty a week before than the Cuban flag.

'Tomorrow is the start of the Spring Festival in Vietnam,' Áspera pointed out. 'It would be nice to get a new flag for that.'

'I've never bought a flag,' the history lecturer replied. 'I don't even know if they still sell them. That one out there has been in the family since I was a kid. True, it wasn't used much in the past.'

'It shouldn't be too difficult or expensive to get one. Let me phone Georgina.'

Georgina was the local equivalent of the *Yellow Pages*. Áspera consulted her for a couple of minutes then returned with a smile that spelt feminine satisfaction in the face of masculine inadequacy.

'You see how easy that was? She says they sell flags for five pesos in the big store on the corner. The one painted green. She bought one recently and it turned out to be good value for money.'

The history lecturer shrugged and began to get dressed.

'I'll go,' Áspera said. 'Men are no good at shopping.'

Carefully she began to fold the flag up. Before long it was just a big lump.

'If I put it in the wardrobe, I'll have to take all your clothes out. This is what's wrong with living in Alamar.[3] We better throw it away.'

'Flags cannot be thrown away. They're burned.'

'Who says so?'

'Everyone knows that. For a national emblem, only fire is pure enough.'

'Sounds like a rule only a man could have came up with. Look at the size of the thing! If we had a dirt yard out back we might be able to burn it. But this is the third floor. Even if we did it on the balcony, do you want ash to be flying around covering everything white, or soot staining the ceiling? Can you deduce who might have to clean up that mess? No, wrap it in an old newspaper and throw it out.'

'I can't. It's just not done. It's unpatriotic.'

Áspera saw herself as a patient woman. But her husband's lack of initiative made her boil like a coffee percolator.

'I'll tell you what's patriotic! Patriotic is that little woman across the street, the deputy minister's mistress, who changes her flag every three or four months. And I'll tell you another thing: I reckon that man brings flags back from abroad, they're always so perfect-looking and brand-new. Don't we have the right to a nice, big, flag of high artistic quality, like her?'

'In terms of flags, quality can only refer to things like the strength of the fabric or the durability of the pigments,' the husband meditated. 'I mean, we are not talking about a design that leaves a lot of room for creative interpretation. You can't have different combinations of colours or replace the straight stripes with wavy ones, nor can you add more stars, or change the factory brand of the dye. It shouldn't cost more just because it's an imported edition, or handmade, or comes with a signature. There can't be a new range, or a special collection, every year. The flag is a unique model, universal and unisex.'

'Keep talking shit,' Áspera interjected, 'that way we'll never win the TV.' [4]

'Okay, okay,' the reserve lieutenant surrendered. 'When I get back with the new one, I will get rid of it.'

'No, I don't want to look at it anymore. I need to be able to breathe. Take it out now.'

'But what if…?'

'Now.'

The Party member didn't dare protest any further. After giving his wife the five pesos, he set about wrapping the flag as respectfully as he could in the pages of a Soviet magazine comprised of strong, opaque paper, then tied it together with thick cord. He left the apartment sporting the most confident air he could muster, and toured the block a couple of times before honing in on some dustbins.

Quiet, he told himself. *A faded, threadbare flag desecrated by cockroaches cannot fulfil the function it was designed for.*

He tried to look at it this way: few acts could be more patriotic than replacing an old flag. There was an allegory for youth here, for the new generation about to step into the shoes of the veterans to continue their work. It is true that cremation is the proper procedure, but isn't it cruel? Didn't Hatuey die by fire,[5] and Joan of Arc, Giordano Bruno also?[6] This way, like everything else deposited in the garbage, will it not be returning to the earth? Will it not become part of the very soil of the motherland? What better destination can a flag have than to become one with the body of the nation?

The dustbins were of the European model, with a narrow mouth and removable lid which the local council had had screwed down to avoid being stolen. Two were full to the brim, but there seemed to be space in the third. The Party member inserted the package, but failed to get more than a few centimetres of it in. He pushed, nervously realising that a neighbour was approaching carrying a bucket swarming with flies. He pushed harder. The bloody flag just wouldn't go in. In the end, out of desperation, he pushed so hard he could have buried a corpse in the Sahara. With a groan, the package buckled and took up its place in the dustbin. The history lecturer immediately stepped aside, and the neighbour emptied his bucket into the bin's mouth. It was a retired lieutenant colonel, a political commissar of the CDR.[7]

'Morning,' said the newcomer, glancing at the monstrous object stuck in the middle of the dustbin. 'Makes you feel guilty, doesn't it?

'Excuse me?'

'Every time I do a spring clean I get rid of furniture, dishes, clothes I don't need. And then I feel guilty. After all, they served me well, right? They were almost a part of me. It's like a betrayal, know what I mean?'

It was just talk, the history lecturer repeated to himself on the way home. The guy was just being sociable. He didn't see anything. He didn't see that corner of the flag sticking out of the ripped newspaper. And even if he had, how could he have known what it was? It was tightly wrapped cloth, a curtain, a quilt, or an old carpet, for all he knew. *Breathe. Everything is fine. Nothing happened.*

He opened the front door, smiling.

'They were out of flags,' Áspera announced.

The party member struggled to rise above this new setback.

'But Georgina told you they had flags! Did you ask if they were expecting a new delivery?'

'Oh, yes, they're waiting. Been waiting for two weeks. They explained that the CDR regularly buys them in bulk to distribute themselves, so they don't always have them in stock. They should arrive soon though.'

'When?'

'I dunno. Soon.'

He drank a glass of water. It wouldn't go down. He had to send down a piece of bread with it, as a chaperone.

'What about you? Did everything go well?'

He said it had. He refused to fall into the trap of putting the blame on his wife. Naturally, she would jump on the defensive. No, the key lay in downplaying the whole thing. Of course, if the commissar asked about the old flag, if he needed evidence come the writ of *habeas corpus*... but hey, what was he thinking! This wasn't one of those countries. Lots of people failed to ever hang flags out the front of their homes. In a few days, new flags will be delivered to the shop. Or he could ask other stores. He would go on Saturday, without fail.

'Calm down,' Áspera told him when he returned from the college at nine o'clock that evening. 'Everything is fine.'

'Everything?'

'Yeah. Well, Georgina called. She wanted to know if we had bought the new flag.'

'What did you say?'

'The truth. That there were no flags. Then she asked me about the old one. I told her I took it in to shake the dust off it.'

The husband shrugged. Yes, that was a sensible answer, half true, half false. Perhaps he was right, after all, and the ex-military guy had seen nothing.

'Oh, also, they left a message under the door. Well, maybe it wasn't a message.'

'Was it or wasn't it? What did it say?'

'That's the problem. It was just a blank sheet of paper.'

The next morning, the lecturer didn't go to work. Peering through a half-opened window, he spotted the political commissar pass in front of the house twice, staring malevolently at the stained, now naked wall. In the afternoon someone had the bright idea to call and then hang up. It happened three times; the fourth was Augustine, phoning from work. He had to go in. There was a Party committee meeting.

Come Saturday, he spent the day trawling all the general stores, the hardware stores, stationery shops, and even a house renting costumes. There were no flags. But there would be soon; that much was certain.

'The commissar of the CDR asked after you,' Áspera said at nine o'clock that evening, as she poured him a bitter, reheated, coffee. 'I told him you'd be back around this time.'

'We're so screwed,' he moaned and related the entire encounter at the dustbin. 'He knows, the bastard knows. He's playing with us, torturing me because he knows. That blank paper was his doing.'

'Maybe it was just a summons to an ordinary committee meeting which got misprinted and came out white. He always brings them. It would be a funny week if he didn't...'

A knock sounded at the door. The history lecturer looked at his wife with despair. She prayed silently, while he didn't feel it appropriate to defer to the mystical content of an obscurantist religion. He told himself that if prayer served for anything, the visitor would turn out to be someone else: a child perhaps, an aunt, a neighbour asking for salt. Áspera opened the door. It was the commissar.

'I'll bring you coffee,' she said before the ex-military man could open his mouth. 'Just made it fresh. Delicious. A cousin of mine sent it from Baracoa.'

The newcomer thanked her, and uttered a few innocuous remarks about the heat and North American madness. Only when he had tasted and approved the coffee, and Áspera had excused herself, saying she had things to do in the kitchen, did he turn on his victim, armed with all the details.

'My best friend died in Girón.'[8]

'I'm sorry,' the husband offered. He knew this wasn't exactly news, but rather a preamble to something else. Now that it had started, he almost felt relief.

'He died defending the flag. He preferred to stain it with his blood than allow it to fall into enemy hands. There are schools and factories bearing his name now.'

There followed an immeasurable silence.

'More coffee?' asked the husband. His interrogator declined, looking into his eyes as if trying to decode his handiwork.

'Why did you do this? How you can you besmirch your

homeland like that? You know what my friend would say if he were alive?'

'I didn't mean to defile anything. The flag was in a state of disrepair.'

The military man swore and spoke of purifying fire. Not for the first time, the husband felt the temptation to inform on his wife, and spare no detail. And also not for the first time he restrained himself. What he did, instead, was spell out his theory about Hatuey and Joan of Arc, and the concept of the flag's remnants transforming into the flesh of the nation.

'Stop trying to complicate things with the French and the Dominicans. I believe you threw it away as an act of political provocation.'

'Ask Georgina! We told her that we thought we would buy another flag. So we threw the old one away!'

'I already did. You told her that you'd removed our national flag for washing. If you lied about one thing, I don't see why you wouldn't lie about another. But suppose you really did want to replace it. Explain to me why you threw out the old one without having bought the new one.'

The image of four spooked horses dismembering his wife, limb from limb, passed through the lecturer's mind, only with Christmas music playing in the background.[9] With an effort he erased the beatific scene. His only choice was to go on the offensive. With a bold, desperate, Napoleonic sortie.

'It wasn't like that. *We already have a new flag.*'

'Lie! There's none in the store. Georgina told me...'

'We wanted to surprise everyone. The one we have now is the greatest, the most beautiful...'

'Show it to me.'

'Listen, I'm a Party member. A revolutionary. I participated in the Literacy Campaign. In fact, I *taught* my own wife to read. You cannot walk in here and doubt my word...'

The retired lieutenant colonel came so close he could

almost feel the rasp of those sharp hairs sticking out of his nose.

'Listen, I won't insist right now. I consider myself a just man, and I thought a lot before coming over here tonight. I think even you deserve a second chance. That's what my friend would have wanted.'

The lecturer nodded emphatically, as if he too had known the hero of the Bay of Pigs and could attest that the CDR man had interpreted his thinking correctly.

'Next Tuesday... you know what that day represents. There will be a parade, parties and joy in the streets. And flags, from simple chains of paper flags to large, canvas ones. One way or another, the national flag will be present in all revolutionary houses.' He took a finger to Áspera's husband's chest and poked it threateningly: 'Hang your big, beautiful new flag out of your window that day, and I promise that no one will know of this incident. But if you don't, I swear to you by Antonio Maceo, I will break both your legs.'

Then he left.

Sunday morning came and the lecturer phoned every friend and relative he could think of. Then he rose and got dressed.

'No one can lend me a flag. Either they don't have one, or they need theirs for Tuesday, or it's "No, and that's final." I would say no myself. Calling to ask for a flag sounds like a provocation.'

'Where are you going?'

'To see Augustine. As secretary of the Party's technical committee for the college, he must have one. He is my friend. He won't say no to me.'

'And if he doesn't lend it to you?

'Well, a meteorite could drop on my head as well. My God, Áspera,' he paused. '"God"? Look what you've made me say now. Augustine is my last chance.'

'Don't be late.'

'You think I'm going on a picnic? Augustine lives in San Augustin.'

It took the professor nearly two hours to get to the house of the committee secretary. He found him under the Lada, covered in oil.

'Of course, I will lend it to you, brother,' Augustine said, expansively. 'You don't have to explain anything. Otherwise tell me, what good is it being a communist, if you don't help others? That was what Che taught me. He even gave me a keychain once, you know.'

His wife served coffee – a close relative of the one Áspera had made for him. Then they talked about the heat and North American madness. And finally Augustine handed him the flag.

'You know you have to bring it back to me on Wednesday. I don't want anyone to think...'

'Of course,' said the lecturer.

That night Áspera and her husband dined like royalty. They even treated themselves to a bar of *Peters* chocolate that they'd bought in Lenin Park two months before. Then they watched television and made love one and a half times.

'We are buying ourselves some time with this,' he told Áspera, as they lit two different cigarettes – his Popular, hers Aroma. 'Then we'll have to squat at the store, until the new flags come in...'

'I'll take care of that,' Áspera reassured him. 'I'll buy the best one they have and from then on it will always stay out.'

'No,' mused her husband out loud. 'This has all happened to us because we were *too* patriotic. If we had never hung the flag out in the first place, no one would insist we hang one out now. From now on we are going to approach this with moderation.'

'Even this? You mean..?'

'This.'

On Monday, the Party member went to work and the classes he gave were somewhat cynical in tone, by his standards. Meanwhile, Áspera brushed the flag, and even sprayed a little perfume on it.

At night a knock came at the door: it was Augustine's wife, inconsolable.

'My husband had a heart attack.'

'This can't be,' his best friend responded. 'He was just fine today.'

'Well,' said the wife, 'he is dead, and I need the flag for the funeral.'

Áspera fainted.

'No!' the lecturer wailed. 'Augustine, don't do this shit to me!'

'I'll pretend I didn't hear that,' the widow whispered. 'Give me the flag. He always wanted to be wrapped in it when the time came.'

'Flags are meant to be burned!' the reserve lieutenant insisted.

Leaving the wake early, the moment he could get away from the relatives of the deceased and his workmates, the history lecturer went straight to the house of a bootlegger he had been at primary school with.

'People come to me asking for drugs, porno magazines, American clothes! Once a deputy minister asked me for some real snow for his daughter's fifteenth birthday party because the girl wanted to make a snowman with a carrot nose. But, a Cuban flag? This is hard. You should give me three days' notice at least, man.'

'I need it before dawn.'

'Look, the best I can do you right now is an Almendares club flag. I know a mate who must still have a national flag, but an old one, from the time of the *mambises*,[10] with a white square, and a red one...'

The lecturer was picked up by the police at five o'clock the following morning. The officer on duty found it suspicious that this individual was talking to himself maniacally, while clutching a bulging briefcase to his chest. The briefcase turned out to contain fifteen flags of different sizes. He didn't know, or would not say, where he had taken them from and what he planned to do with them, so he was taken to the station. There he was locked up for a couple of days, before being interned at the Havana Psychiatric Hospital, to be released a year later.

In the 80s, the political commissar of the Comités de Defensa de la Revolución took refuge in the Peruvian embassy.[11] He now lives in Atlanta.

The history lecturer passed away in October, 1986, his last words being: 'I want them to be buried with me.' In November that year, Áspera began getting permanent work as an extra in the state film industry.

Notes

1. Taken from the well-known patriotic poem 'En menudos pedazos' by the nineteenth century Cuban poet Bonifacio Byrne: 'Si deshecha en menudos pedazos/ Llega a estar mi bandera algún día/ Nuestros muertos, alzando los brazos/ La sabrán defender todavía' (If one day my flag/ is torn into tiny pieces/ our dead heroes, raising their arms,/ will still defend it).

2. José Julián Martí Pérez (1853-1895); an internationally renowned author, journalist, poet and politician, a key figure in the planning and execution of the Cuban War of Independence (1895-1898); he died in combat at the beginning of the conflict. Much venerated, as a national hero, by all Cubans, no matter their political orientation.

3. Alamar; the largest public housing project in Cuba, known for its Soviet-style prefab architecture, part of the municipio of Habana del Este, in an eastern district of the city.

4. In Cuba, after the Revolution of 1959, television sets and other electronic equipment were given to workers for merit, by the workers' assembly. If you did more voluntary labour in the neighbourood, for example, you might be awarded a television.

5. Hatuey (died 1512), was a Taíno cacique, or chief, originally from the island of Hispaniola, who lived in the early sixteenth century and fled to Cuba during the Spanish conquest. He has attained legendary status for leading a group of natives in a fight against the invading Spaniards, and thus becoming one of the first fighters against colonialism in the New World. He is celebrated as 'Cuba's First National Hero'.

6. Giordano Bruno (1548 –1600), an Italian Dominican friar, poet, philosopher and mathematician. Burned at the stake for his Copernican cosmological theories.

7. The CDR: *Comités de Defensa de la Revolución*, the revolutionary defence committees, based in each community.

8. In April 1961, Playa Girón was one of two landing sites for seaborne forces of about 1,500 armed Cuban exiles in the Bay of Pigs Invasion, an American CIA-sponsored attempt to overthrow the new government of Cuban Prime Minister Fidel Castro. Over 72

hours, fighting took place in many parts of the Cienaga de Zapata, Playa Girón being the last remaining area occupied by the invaders.

9. An allusion to José Gabriel Túpac Amaru (1738–1781), known as Túpac Amaru II, the leader of a large Andean uprising against the Spanish in Peru, the quelling of which resulted in his execution: dismemberment by four horses, which having failed, was followed by his body being quartered, and beheaded on the main plaza in Cuzco (in the same place his apparent great-great-great-grandfather Túpac Amaru I had also been beheaded).

10. Guerrilla Cuban independence soldiers who fought against Spain in the Ten Years' War (1868–78) and the Cuban War of Independence (1895–98).

11. A possible reference to The Mariel Boatlift − a mass emigration of Cubans, who travelled from Cuba's Mariel Harbour to the United States between 15 April and 31 October 1980.

Love in the Big City

Eduardo Heras León

For Ambrosio Fornet

HE JUST TOLD ME. *He just said his piece and off he went. Turned his back and walked away. I had to say something but suddenly I realised I couldn't think what. So he left. Who knows where he was heading. Probably even he didn't know. There were so many destinations in this city. 'Don't lose yourself' was the one thing I had told him the last time we'd seen each other, almost two years ago, during his trip to Havana.*

They had knocked on my door – him and his friend, Germán. They were both dirty, hungry and happy. The three of us ate eggs and rice and two old pieces of bread. He recited poems and spoke of Guantánamo:

We had to visit! We just had to! Who's ever going to appreciate two tramps in sandals talking about poetry back there? 'What's that? An earring! Here, in the land of General Periquito Pérez?[1] Never seen anything like it! Young men wearing earrings in the hot weather of Guaso, the birthplace of Policarpo Pineda, aka Rustán,[2] "more beast than man", as the Apostle says?'[3] Who would understand that, eh, Comrade? And what they don't understand, they won't tolerate. And what they won't tolerate, they persecute. That's what happens out there, in the provinces. But what can you do? If they persecute you, and if you refuse to take your earring out, cut your hair, or change your sandals for sport shoes – for designer trainers – because you don't have enough cuc[4] or even enough dollars to do so, even if you wanted to, and because you're not going to wear the shoes they give you with the Libreta,[5] because they feel like shit, you get me – then what? Either you leave, or they make your life impossible... that's-the-question, *asere*.[6] Someone once told me, I'm not a fucking barber nor a shoemaker, so I don't know anything about long hair or sandals. For me, it's simple: short hair and well-shod feet, that's one thing, anything else makes you a homosexual, and if you throw in poetry, it's even worse, that makes you a fag. Do you copy me, brother?

So, what's the solution? You come to Havana. To escape the miserable, daily oppression of a job you can't stand, or the apathy you feel towards a job you don't even have, to spare yourself the long nights sitting in the park, looking at the same faces, saying the same things, inventing ways to kill the spare time you have, because that time doesn't go anywhere, doesn't move on; it's not the sort of time you can fill with literature or theatre or the illusion of becoming a sculptor can fill. Because back there in the provinces you can tell you're just going round in circles, spinning around an axis that's wearing out and nobody can be bothered to fix. No one will do it. We are sure of that. And so you come to Havana.

You're young. Who doesn't like adventure, or the freedom a big city has to offer? So you press the eject button. You set off with nothing but your bus fare, a few cigarettes, and some bread with something scraped over it. The bus terminal is an anthill; there's a waiting list, an endless queue; two days should be enough time to get a seat. You can't sleep. You can just about piss; shitting is impossible. Bathing a distant dream. But this time you're lucky: they put on an extra coach; the announcement takes people by surprise, but not you; you stay alert, and jump on board. The coach starts. 'Fuck you, small town!'

★

It was 20 hours on the road, when I came for good. Each town with a sadness so similar to my own. Were they always like that? I was sticky with sweat, and hungry the whole night through. Dawn approached, but no lights. Where were those famous lights of Havana? Beyond the well-lit terminal they drop me off at, a forest of shadows waited for me: the mouth of a great wolf I was about to throw myself into, because I have no other choice. Heaving my backpack over my shoulder, I set out along Avenida de Rancho Boyeros, to what I later learned was Carlos III. Someone came up behind me and in no time overtook me.

'Do you come from the East?'

'*Yeah.*' I looked at him. He was about 50; short, fat, his voice faint, almost a whisper. 'And... where are you going?'

I looked at him again.

'I mean, only if you want to tell me.'

'I don't know.'

'Of course, you don't have anywhere to go, right?'

A shy smile. 'Even so, what's it to you?'

'Nothing, nothing, don't get annoyed. I was waiting for a relative who didn't turn up.'

'So...' This time I looked at him seriously. 'If you don't mind...'

I almost burst out laughing.

And so, the first chapter began: *OLD HAVANA FAG WANTS TO FUCK YOUNG GUANTÁNAMO GUAJIRO.*[7]

'I have an empty bed at home you can use tonight, no charge.'

'And why me? Seeing as you don't even know me?'

'Ah, you see, these things happen in life. I like you.'

I didn't say any more.

Neither did he.

A strange sense of complicity suddenly descended on me which I couldn't shake off. Or didn't know how to. I followed his steps as if carried along by inertia. We arrived, after a few minutes, at what turned out to be a small apartment. And as I sat on his couch, I felt strangely safe, a rare moment of peace. My adventure was off to a good start. He told me his name was Carlos. Apparently he was very content; I would even say happy. He let me take a bath, gave me some food, put soft music on, and before I fell asleep, I had no option, I let him touch me a little!

I only stayed a few days. Carlos started to get silly and tried to take other liberties that a roof and a meal wouldn't compensate. I didn't think twice about leaving. Maybe if I had, I would still be in that house. Because, you know, it wasn't so bad there: I ate every day; it was safe; and ultimately the old man only pestered me at night. He was content, at least at first, with the small things I let him do. And let's be clear: I am no fag, nor am I a *buga*.[8] Of course, there are times when I don't really care where pleasure comes from; I accept it no questions asked. No hang-ups. But the truth is, I was getting bored of the routine I'd fallen into: I was going out very little, just the odd short walk to get used to a city that seemed monstrous to me, that overwhelmed me sometimes, made me feel dizzy. The rest of the time I spent at home watching videos – the old man had a top-of-the-range Sony. That was it. But I hadn't migrated to Havana just to become the companion of some old headcase. So, on the fourth or fifth night, I can't remember which, under some pretext, I picked up the few clothes I had, stuffed them into my backpack and made for the door. Carlos got up and handed me a ten peso note, telling me I could come back any time I wanted. I stared at him. I had an urge to tell him to fuck off, to be mean to him, make fun of him. But oddly, all I felt was pity. Or was it fondness? Look at it this way;

what right did I have to insult him? Had he not been good to me? Had he not fed me for practically nothing in return? All I could do was laugh and pat him on the back as if saying goodbye to an old friend. After all, isn't that what he was?

I walked up to the Coppelia.[9] I had discovered it on one of my little walks and learned how much it deserved its reputation: all roads lead to the Coppelia. Nearby, in a dark corner close to the bus stop, a group of teenagers were hanging out of the railings, whispering to each other. Their clothes caught my attention: frayed jeans ripped in several places, and instead of shirts, many wore strips of leather sewn together. Their hair was outrageously long; like Red Indians, with a band of cloth tied around their foreheads. I leaned against the railing, watching them for some time. It seemed they didn't notice me. I decided to try my luck in the queue for the ice cream and started walking away. Someone called me. I turned. A girl from the group came up to me. She showed me a cigarette.

'Do you have a match?'

'I do.'

She lit the cigarette. 'Are you alone?'

'I am.'

'Not from Havana?'

'No.'

'Wanna hang with us?'

'Why not.'

She took my hand and we headed over to the group.

'He's not from here,' she said. Then, laughing: 'He talks in monosyllables.'

I took out a pack of cigarettes and offered them round: several eager hands reached forward.

'Why don't we go to the Cubicle?' said a tall, thin guy they called Rafa.

'With him?' Another of them said.

'Why not, Rony?' she shot back.

They all got up. She took my hand. 'Come on. I'm Marisela. You?'

'Hubert.'

'Where you from?'

'Guantánamo.'

'Do you like Pink Floyd? Hey? Don't you listen to music?'

'Yes.'

'Hard rock? Heavy metal?'

'No.'

'So what do you like?'

'The Beatles.'

She grimaced. 'What else?'

'Cuban music.'

'Shit, don't mention that crap here. I like you though. You just need teaching a few things first, you uncultured *guajiro* – so you can make it to heaven with me, you'll see!'

And I did see, of course. Who couldn't see with Marisela? She took me to heaven with her too. All that night, in her sanctuary, sharing a bottle with the rest of the group, after swallowing the pill she'd put in my mouth that set me on a journey of no return. I floated, weightless; torn in two, detached from my body, like some mystical entity looking down on the whole group, surprised to discover myself down there, hugging Marisela. I heard the sound of bells and, in the distance, her voice, and the voices of everyone else speaking simultaneously, and after that violent music, a ruthless rhythm that swept up everything in a dizzying crescendo. Then I lost all sense of reality. When I woke up, my head pounding, we were in bed together – with her asleep beside me in the smallest of rooms. We were naked and suddenly I felt as if I were no more than a helpless, shivering creature, my body shaking with a chill deep in my bones. I pressed myself against her and she began to stretch lazily. I barely had time to change position before she jumped on top of me and frantically began sucking on my lips, prompting a violent erection that she mounted and used to drive into her furiously until she couldn't last any longer, letting out a scream like a violated animal followed by an almost endless sigh and a shudder that only faded away slowly. I could hear the fast pace of her breathing begin to settle till it was no more than a whisper. Then I grabbed her gently by the shoulders, freeing her from my body, and setting her on her hands and knees with her back to me. I gripped her waist, squeezing so that her buttocks began to open up before me. When I began to enter her there, she tried to protest, but then she opened wider and I pushed, entering her eventually with difficulty, at first letting out a dull moan that grew in intensity. Before long she was biting the pillow and suddenly, breathless and distraught, she shouted, 'More!' I grabbed her by the armpits and with all my strength penetrated her completely; her screams mingled with mine until they subsided into gasping breaths, soft spasms, tenderness and that delicious torpor which wraps everything in the mists of sleep.

I lived in that room with Marisela for several weeks, every day an exact replica of the one that went before. Each morning and afternoon we'd repeat the same sequence – bed-bath-lunch-bed-snack-bed-bath-bed – till night fell and then hit the town, with the group, ending the session in the Cubicle. I endured that claustrophobic atmosphere, with the same dialogue, the same music, the same voices that, at first, I had rejected, but whose very monotony I now felt was essential as if fully integrated into this strange brotherhood, so alien to my nature.

One day, no different from the rest, Rafa arrived at the club, his face flushed with excitement. He gathered Rony,

Michael, Yosi, and Ena around him, whispering, until laughter drowned out whatever they were saying. Then they came over to us.

'We are going to offer you a great honour,' Rafa began, smiling.

'What honour?' asked Marisela suspiciously.

'You're going to be the first of us to inject it.'

'What am I going to inject?' I said, laughing.

'The HIV,'[10] Rafa said seriously.

'Ah, fuck you!,' I said still jokingly.

'No kidding, *guajiro*. We are all going to do it and we are going to start with you, you're the rookie of the year.'

'What, are you crazy? Are they crazy?'

'We're going to die anyway, peasant, so what does it matter if it's now or later?' Rafa said, suddenly producing a syringe containing two or three centimetres of blood. 'At least we'll have some fun.' Yosi and Michael began to move. Marisela tried to stand in front of me, to protect me.

'Move aside, Ena, this is nothing to do with you.'

'Rafa, drop this shit. What the fuck's happened to you!'

'Get out of the way, damn it, or you'll be the first!' Rafa was closing in, threateningly, his eyes blazing, as if on something.

I was paralysed, not knowing whether it was out of fear, or some panic attack. But Marisela's gesture made me react. I didn't think twice.

'Fuck your mother!' – I yelled, lunging at him with a right hook to the face. I didn't give him time to react. I leapt towards the door, opened it with a jerk, and ran out into the night, leaving Marisela's cries to trickle into the street behind me. I don't know how long I ran for, or what streets I passed through. My head was ready to explode and I almost passed out. I couldn't run anymore. Finally I stopped in a park and collapsed on a bench. Fear and disgust boiled inside me, mixed with an immense sense of weariness and an uncontrollable urge to cry. I cried for all the days I'd spent in this incomprehensible city learning about nothing but the dark side of life, the city's rotten teeth. I cried at the image of a landscape in ruins populated by ignoble beings, unquiet spirits searching for the death that would deliver them. I had never felt more alone. I settled myself on that bench, almost without thinking, and lay there motionless, tears trickling down my face, until I'd lost all track of time. Suddenly I heard a murmur that quickly amplified into a hoarse voice. Someone was grabbing me by the shirt. I opened my eyes. It was daylight. How many hours had passed? I stood up. A face stared at me cruelly.

'Identity card, Citizen!'

I can't remember what story I told that cop but, despite his brusque manner, he ended up simply warning me: not to fall back to sleep, if I didn't want everything, down to my socks, stolen from me, and that next time he would have to take me down to the station. Depressed and hungry, I set off down the first avenue that appeared to me and suddenly the open door of a church, huge and silent, seemed to offer itself as refuge.

I had never been inside a church. My parents were atheists, or at least never talked about religion. Back in Guantánamo, there might have been times when I paused in front of a village chapel to watch the bride coming out, but I'd never had any curiosity to go in. Now, strangely, I felt compelled to stop and walk towards this grand, stone edifice opening up to me, I felt drawn towards a space which, without knowing how, began to wrap me in its serenity. I didn't think twice as I gently pushed the door wider. The gloom of the place and the unaccustomed silence broken only by the echo of distant footsteps somehow managed to calm me. Before me was a space in shadow, dimly lit by sunlight softened by the stained-glass windows, and rising in a marvel of symmetries and spirals only to lose itself at a point beyond the reach of these eyes, darkened as they have been by so much loneliness. My vision became blurred. Overwhelmed by fatigue, and on the verge of collapsing, I reached out and grabbed hold of what at first seemed a piece of wood, but whose smooth texture, almost polished, made me look up. It was Christ on the cross, but a different Christ, an athletic one, full of energy, a far cry from the traditional, ascetic figure: more human than divine.

'My son, don't touch the Lord's body,' a voice spoke behind me.

I turned my head, instinctively retracting my hand.

'Sorry, Father, it's just I almost fainted. I didn't mean...'

'Do you feel unwell?'

'Not so much now. I just got dizzy.'

'Come, sit here,' he said as he took me by the shoulder and led me to one of the pews.

He was a tall thin priest with large, well-manicured hands. He looked about 40, though he may have been a little older.

'It looks like you need help,' he said, sitting down next to me. 'Or am I wrong?'

I looked up and stared at him. Suddenly, it was as if a wave of infinite goodness had just washed over me. I couldn't stop the unbearable pressure tightening in my chest; my eyes filled with tears, and I cried helplessly reaching over to the shoulder this priest was offering me as refuge. I cried long and hard, my sobbing eventually trailing off as a strange peace settled inside me. The priest handed me a handkerchief.

'Do you want me to hear your confession?'

'No, I've never done it, I prefer to talk to you, but not here.'

'Do you want to come to my house? We won't be disturbed there.'

So we made our way there in silence. Almost upon arrival, he asked me my name and where I came from. When I told him, he smiled saying we were almost neighbours. He was born in Holguin. His name was Victor. He lived in an apartment near the church, discreetly yet comfortably furnished. I noticed a very sophisticated sound system and a huge collection of cassettes and CDs. He saw me looking and smiled

'It's almost all classical music, plus some jazz and slow rock. I don't like music that's too loud. But, sit, sit.' He went into a room and reappeared a few minutes later without the cassock.

'You are calmer now. Come on, tell me, that's why I am here, to help you spiritually, in so far as I can.'

There was something in his voice, a subtlety, a quiet intonation, a soothing serenity that helped create an atmosphere of confidence and unfamiliar human warmth. I began to feel better, nervously at first. Then I calmly told him everything – day by day, almost minute by minute – not quite realising what I was saying, without hiding anything, not even my most intimate desires: my Havana adventures, the unusual sexual experiences with Carlos and Marisela, the pills and binge drinking, the long nights on weed at the Cubicle, the litany of disgust, routine, boredom, and finally fear – the almost animal terror – that came over me that night that I would never forget. When I finished, the exhilarated tone of my voice surprised me; I stood up, gesticulating at the end of my story. Then, just as quickly, I collapsed back onto the couch. I was sweating.

The priest was silent, his eyes almost closed, lips moving imperceptibly, as if whispering a prayer. When he realised I'd finished, he looked at me.

'Is that it?'

'Doesn't it sound like much to you?'

'No, neither too much nor too little. It's just, the state you were in when you came to the church, I thought it would be worse.'

I looked at him very seriously.

'Father, it was really scary. These people are crazy, who

would dream of injecting someone with a disease like AIDS?'

'True, my son, but things like that happen in this country. There is such a loss of values, many young people become lost. They are the most vulnerable, the weakest, precisely because of their youth. But don't fool yourself. Compared to others I know, these adventures of yours are just skirmishes, things that can happen to anyone like you who sets out to conquer the capital, to hijack it – isn't that how you say it?'

I smiled. Where did Father Victor get these expressions from? He seemed to guess what I was thinking.

'Don't be surprised. I have listened to many young people like you. I know things about this world you couldn't imagine. You see? What you have just finished doing is nothing more than a confession, as we understand it. And therefore' – he raised his right hand and made the sign of the cross in the air – '*ego te absolvo a peccatis tuis in nomine Patris et Filii et Spiritus Sancti.*'

He got up, went into the kitchen, and a few minutes later returned with a tray of milk, bread and butter, little treasures that I had forgotten all about. After breakfast, he came up with a proposal. He wanted me to help him with his paperwork, he would teach me how to use the computer – he had one installed in his bedroom – I could learn how to use the word processor. I would copy articles, materials he prepared for I-don't-know-what newsletter and other provincial publications.

For the moment I could live there, he would put a camp bed with a mattress in the room. Nobody would bother me, I would have a key to the house. So... what do you think? How could I not accept? How could I refuse? All is not lost, I thought. There are still people who make it all worthwhile.

Two weeks later, the computer held no secrets from me. I would rise early each morning, make coffee in almost complete silence, and sneak into Father Victor's room, to switch on the computer and start working. Half an hour later, he would wake and in a few minutes would be ready to go; we'd exchange a few greetings happily before he left for work. I never really knew what he did there, as I never asked him. At noon he would come back, and we'd lunch together. He went out again, and when he returned, at about six o'clock, I would have cleaned the house and finished the other small tasks I had adopted from day one. During that time I almost never went out at night. I preferred to listen to music, or watch a video – Father Victor had the very latest Philips VHS – or I just read the computer manuals that I found lying around. He never went out either. Instead he stayed home listening to music with me, reviewing the materials I'd typed, or simply reading the Bible. Within two weeks, I received my first wages and I had the feeling I was finally a happy young man, that the priest was the father figure I had never known, and that, if there was any justice on Earth, time would stop here, in these beautiful, innocent days, to compensate somehow for the horror of what had passed before. I felt so protected, so safe from all the miseries of the world. I started to change also; my language softened and, for the first time since I arrived, the need for art and beauty gripped my senses. At one point, I even got my hands on some clay and shaped an ashtray for him, leaving it, without saying anything, on his desk. Father Victor did not try to preach to me; religion seemed to be more than just a way of making a living, for him, but a deeply-rooted conviction, an attitude towards people and the world.

Exactly one month in, on the day of my second pay cheque, we made a special dinner together. I took a chance and bought a bottle of rum to celebrate. He told me he did not want to drink, it was not good for him. But I insisted, and we finished the bottle happily, singing old trova[11] songs and even some Beatles' tunes, as we drank. I'm not sure how the night ended. I was almost unconscious by the end, but I vaguely remember Father Victor helping me undress and putting me in his own bed, despite my feeble protests. I must have passed out instantly. I do not remember dreaming. It was a deep, primitive, refreshing sleep. But come morning, a soft caress was slowly drawing me from this vague and distant place; it was a very slight touch, as if someone were running a bird's feather down my neck, shoulders and chest, finally ending at a place where my whole body became aroused. The mists of sleep were dissipating and I felt that delicious tingle up and down my chest reaching almost to the tip of my sex, which roused to a full erection. Still half asleep I stroked it with my hand for a moment, then suddenly I woke up. On opening my eyes, Father Victor seemed very close to the bed, and was staring at me with an unknowable intensity. I was completely naked and, seeing him, only half-covered myself with the sheet. Father Victor did not move. A few long, drawn-out seconds passed. Then I got out of the bed, grabbed my clothes, walked past him without looking at him, and locked myself in the bathroom. I turned on the shower. The cold water did me good. When I came out, hair combed and dressed, I went to the closet, pulled out some clothes, stuffed them in my old backpack, and only then turned to Father. He sat on the edge of the bed, his head in his hands, in silence.

'Victor, I'm going,' I said abruptly.

He looked up at me intensely. 'It's not what you think. You don't have to leave.'

From the door, I regarded him sadly. He held my gaze, then outstretched his arms to me. I was about to lose myself in them, to once more seek the warmth of a refuge that seemed my birthright. But I couldn't.

I was surprised how calmly I left and made my way into the infernal noise of that newly awakened city. I wandered through its streets, walked along the Malecón, talked with fishermen, with delinquent children, with sleepy whores returning from their nocturnal hunting, with tourists who had been up all night and others still insatiably searching for pleasure.

I do not know how much time passed; hours, days, weeks. It was then that I saw you. I had almost forgotten you, and suddenly it seemed to me someone had put you in my way so I could tell you this story. You see, more than two hours on this wall, talking, have only served to cobble together this story of human weakness. I don't want you to say anything, I don't want advice, nor help, not even the pity that already seems to be peeking out of your eyes. Chances are you will tell me the usual thing: 'Don't lose yourself.' And of course not, now I know I'll never lose myself. Do you see that *turistaxi* that's stopped over there, honking insistently? Do you see that tourist waiting to take me wherever I want? Do you think that I can lose myself? No, nothing you say will change anything. We'll meet again. Somewhere.

I wanted to say something, but he didn't let me. Turned his back on me and walked away. Got into the car that sped away like a frightened animal.

Night was falling and the sea was strangely quiet. The city was beginning to turn on its lights. A smell of rotten seafood was rising up out of the bay.

Notes

1. General Pedro Agustín Pérez (1844–1914), aka Periquito Pérez; a general of the Cuban Liberation Army, mayor of Guantánamo, and distinguished military figure in the region during the War of Independence (1895–1898).

2. José Policarpo Pineda Rustán (1839–1872); a colonel who fought in the War for Independence in Guantánamo. Like Periquito Pérez, he is a symbol of national courage and machismo.

3. The 'Apostle' is a reference to poet and national hero, José Martí (1853–1895), often referred to as the Apostle of Cuban Independence. See page 13, Note 2.

4. Cuban Convertible Pesos

5. Libreta: the Libreta de Abastecimiento ('Supplies booklet'), part of the rationing system in Cuba.

6. Asere: mate, buddy.

7. Guajiro: peasant

8. Buga, from 'bugarrón': Cuban slang for a male prostitute, a heterosexual male who, not identifying as homosexual, has sex with men while still engaging in typical sexual activity with women.

9. The most famous ice cream vendor in Havana, in the Vedado neighbourhood.

10. In the 1990s there were cases of young, homeless Cubans injecting themselves with HIV, deliberately, in order to secure places in hospices (as depicted in films like Gerardo Chijona's Boleto al Paraiso (*Ticket to Heaven*).

11. Trova: a popular music song, sung with the guitar.

All Because of that Fucking Spanish Kid

Daniel Chavarria

> *The source of this text, concerning events in Havana in 1997, is an interview I conducted with the mercenary Cruz León[1] while in custody. In adapting his testimony for literary purposes, I have attempted to retain Cruz's Salvadorean vernacular; thus a 'bicho' is a kid, a 'maje' a guy, and a 'chele' is a white woman. Other words can be understood from the context. Not to do so might have ruined the flavour and realism of the story. My thanks go to Elias, a good Salvadorean, who helped me with the lexicon and syntax of the transcript.*
>
> Daniel Chavarria, December 2011.

NO, MAN. NO. KILLING for the sake of killing is bullshit. I'm not one of those sadists who enjoys someone else's suffering. I fell in love with the killing profession after watching *The Day of the Jackal*. That's right, mate, I discovered that this was my calling. And I got so hooked on it, so engrossed in it, that I started to kill for free... Yes for free, in El Salvador, just to learn the craft. And once I'd completed my first few hits, I wanted no other job...

No, no, the one at the carnival and that small-time hit at

the *Two Shows*, were just to screw some rich bitches... As for why? Like anyone else, no? To get a bit of the good life, to make a lot of money, that's why...

Look, what I like is renting planes and parachuting, eating well and leaving tips, and I always thought that when I'd made a lot of dough I would go to Las Vegas, first class of course, and while there fuck a few *cheles*... Yes, that's what we called the milk-white women, who in El Salvador are the most expensive... All of this under the Jackal's direction.

True, he was getting plenty of dosh for every hit...

Me? Nah, peanuts... Only thirty thousand pesos per bomb... Some three thousand five hundred dollars, like...

But, you have to start somewhere...

Let's see if I remember: I bought my mom a music box, fancy towels for my girlfriend, and we locked ourselves away in a five-star hotel for several days...

Yeah, yeah, that's what I did, after my first trip to Cuba. And while there I also enjoyed some great screwing with Cuban girls – who were, as is natural – in hotels with swimming pools... Imagine that...

What? Yes, but, do you know what I like most about my job? It revs you up, it gets you going; I could work for nothing and do it just for the sense of adventure, the danger... That's right, for free...

What are you asking here? Well, at the beginning, killing people for money is not that easy, it depends on where the hit is taking place and what the circumstances are; sometimes you have to work on the street and you think the whole fucking world is staring at you, so you get hesitant, but then after a while, as your confidence grows, you learn to work at your own pace, no rush, and sooner or later you just couldn't care less, because...

No, man, when you are learning, you choose a remote and dark place, and then there is no hesitation...

Yeah, man, you really do find it fun, but when the thing is for money...

No. I imagine that first time, in Guatemala, after shooting the guy three times, I jumped on my motorbike out of my head and almost crashed into a truck... Am I afraid to speak? No, man, I have nothing to lose anyway. My lawyer says they are going to cut my sentence down to thirty years, for sure. And Fidel would gain nothing from executing me, these days the death penalty is against human rights... Me... here? I'm cool, thanks. My future's guaranteed, because when this government falls and the people from Miami take control, they will set me free...

What are you laughing at, motherfucker? I'm on course to be a hero of democracy, a human rights poster boy. But why am I bothering, you don't understand a fuck...

No sir, democracy is where it's at, where everything you'll ever want is available – the good and the bad – there for the taking, and where everything is upside down because flowers grow in mud and plants get fertilised with shit... This is what I like, you see, flowers and shit, and laws, yes sir, laws and work for all, where anyone can get a good job and even Mexican motherfuckers like you can earn a living selling coke to your addict buddies or being a mule for the *Narcos*. And guys like me taking down *christians* for cash. Each according to his ability, but doing what he likes best in life...

Well now, I already explained that to you, asshole...

No. Fuck me. What happened was that after watching *Rambo* and *The Jackal*, all the kids in my neighbourhood wanted to be like them...

No, '*bicho*' is what we call a kid in El Salvador...

Do you remember in the film when the Jackal takes a watermelon the size of a *christian's* head, sits it on a tree and bursts it with that single, final shot? I've watched it seventeen times already... Did I like it? You're shitting me, right? I also liked seeing how fancy the Jackal lives; how he dresses, the cravats he puts around his neck, and his manners at the dinner table. Why couldn't I be a gentleman like him? In a democracy, everything is possible. The first thing I did, to see if I was cold-blooded enough, was to start practising. Yes, that's it, by killing people for free... Once I stole a taxi in San Salvador and drove to Zacamil in broad daylight... No, asshole, when it's dark not even *el putas* would go around this neighbourhood. I waited in a corner, next to a cinema, and the first dummy who came near me, I shot him in the head and...

No, man, first I called him and asked for an address, and while he was still coming towards me I thought, 'Poor bastard, if you only knew'... but then what came out of my mouth was 'Die, asshole, your day has come' and *bang*... watching his head burst open I felt like the Jackal with the watermelon, a real 'pro', you know? It's not that I liked killing. I just wanted to learn things properly and make sure I wouldn't feel fear, or guilt, none of what the priests teach you. From that moment on, I knew that despite not being a Yankee, a Brit, or even blonde like the Jackal, I too could become a high-class hitman...

No, the day after, when I saw the photo of the guy, a university student coming out of his girlfriend's house, I felt nothing at all. In the press, the colour pictures showed the blood quite clearly and the brains which had splattered on a telegraph pole and the wall of a nearby house...

Yes, a few days later I picked off a cyclist. He had stopped next to a Ceiba tree and I blew his head off with a .45. Later, when I learned he was only fourteen and lived with his mum and was the third of five brothers with no nanny, I realised I had done him a favour. And when you think of it, perhaps I did a favour to the Italian too...

Yes, the one I killed with the bomb at the Copacabana...

Yes, yes, it was like a little bird that's dying of the cold until a cow takes a dump on top of it, and the warmth of the shit revives it and it falls asleep. But then by midday the shit has dried solid, and the bird tries to shake itself free, at which point a fox – seeing that the shit is moving – rummages through it, sees the bird and eats it. This teaches you that not everything that shits on you wants to fuck you, and not everything that cleans the shit off you wants to save you. And of course, that it's not wise to move too much when you're in the shit...

Are you laughing? Seriously, this is what happened to that Italian, after all, you tell me, what the fuck was that son of a bitch Italian doing in the hotel anyway, so far from home? If he wanted to travel, why didn't he just travel around Italy – which they say is so beautiful and everyone else goes to visit? Why did he have to travel so far? As *el maestro* Posada Carriles would say, this Italian was in the wrong place at the wrong time. I didn't order that dummy to stand there. *Nothing personal, you understand,*[2] as they say in English... As I was saying, without doubt, I did the asshole on the bike a favour, as I learned later that he had stolen that bike and he was a bit of a wacko anyway since his mother started whoring around. No doubt his older brothers had already fucked him and he was getting his own back on the other kids. So, what's such an unhappy life worth? This is why, I'm telling you: I'm not sentimental, nor do I have any old debts to repay, or have some revenge I want to take for things that happened to me when I was a kid...

Of course I had problems, but I bear no grudge against anyone; nor do I feel what they call 'affection' for anyone either. I believe life is just a jungle: the bigger animals eat the smaller ones, because this is how God set up the whole jigsaw puzzle. That's why you have to take it as it comes and... afterwards? Well, later, when I was sure I could be like the Jackal, I started doing hits professionally...

Of course, for the *Narcos*. Because I was always diligent and serious about my work, one day *el maestro*, Posada Carriles sent for me...

What did you say?... No, that would take too long to tell...

Of course, their training at the induction was excellent...

No, I made no mistakes. It was fucking bad luck, that's all. On that day I planted the first two bombs without a hitch: the first at the Copacabana Hotel, where the Italian died, and the second at the Chateau Miramar. Then, as I was going to plant the third at the Triton Hotel, this fucking Spanish kid got in the way, he was thirteen or fourteen...

That's right, a psychic — the son of sixty thousand bitches...

Yeah, a lanky Spanish brat, holidaying with his family. He figured out what I was going to do, I imagine...

Now don't ask me how. It wasn't written on my forehead that I was gonna plant a bomb...

That's it, I'm telling you, he was no more than fourteen and he was sitting there and as soon as he saw me he fixed me with this stare. You wanna see the dirty look he was giving me. As if he knew what I was planning to do, and you wouldn't believe the terrified face he had on him, as if he had just seen the devil...

No, fucking hell, I was sure that the boy couldn't possibly know what I had in mind so I carried on. As usual, I locked myself in the toilet, assembled my *tamalito*,[3] set the timer for 12.32pm and went to sit in the lobby, in the spot I had chosen. But there he was again, the fucking kid, and he kept staring at me. With him was this good-looking girl, around 20, who I later learned was his sister. At 12.20pm I sat behind them on a sofa pushed up against the wall, well, almost against it. It was there, behind the back of a chair, that I was going to leave the bag...

Yes, a plastic bag from the Duty Free Shop...

Exactly: I had put the bomb inside the bag, ready to go off at 12.32pm and not to draw attention I began to look at some photos of the city's streets I'd taken myself. Would you believe it? That son of a bitch kid turns round in his seat and starts staring at me... I was checking the time, 12.23, 12.25, and he just sits there, his eyes fixed on me. And me, a real bastard, wishing he would just explode into a thousand pieces...

It was all his fault, for being so nosy. At 12.27pm, the minute the kid turned around to speak to his sister, I put the bomb on the floor, behind the back of the sofa, and rushed out the door. I grabbed a taxi right there and took off to the Bodeguita del Medio, where I was going to plant the fourth. At that moment I heard the bang: the bomb at the Chateau had gone off, and at 12.32pm, *BANG*, the one I had just planted at the Triton, and I imagined that son of a bitch of a kid flying, body parts in all directions. But I played dumb and asked the taxi driver about the explosions and the asshole told me they were controlled explosions on a site nearby where they want to build a new hotel. When we reached the traffic lights I saw a policeman with a walkie-talkie signalling to the driver to pull over to the side of the street. The son of a bitch lowered his head to see who was in the car...

Yes, I was shitting myself but outwardly cool, just like in the movies. The guy was scowling at me and I looked him straight in the eye; you can imagine, I was carrying a bomb with me right there, that I was going to plant at the Bodeguita del Medio later on, so if the policeman had decided to search me...

Ah, yes, what happened to the kid? As far as I've been told later, when he saw me leaving, he started to pull his sister by the sleeve telling her I'd planted a bomb and making a fuss and shouting at everyone to run. And suddenly, *BANG*, the bomb goes off. When the Security Forces arrived they started to question the boy and apparently he helped the police draw up a sketch of me that was as good as a photograph...

Yes, a colour photograph and everything, he gave such a detailed description of me, the little fucker, and that same evening I got caught. They brought some motherfucker dogs and the minute they smelled me they started barking...

That's it. It looked like they were going to finish me...

But if the kid hadn't been such a psychic, or so nosy, they would never have got me... That very evening, with no difficulties at all, I had planted my last bomb at the Bodeguita and when I left I sighed with such relief. My mission accomplished, the day after I would have left the country. I already had my plane ticket with Mexicana de Aviacion. But when I arrived at the hotel where I was going to spend the night, the police were there, waiting for me. Truth is, I did everything my instructor told me and made no mistakes. Not a single one. It was just bad fucking luck and that fucking Spanish kid.

Notes

1. In 1997 a series of explosions at various hotels in the Cuban capital, Havana, left one dead (Italian tourist Fabio di Celmo) and 11 injured. Former CIA agent Luis Posada Carriles, born in Cuba but holding a Venezuelan passport, admitted organising the bombing campaign. In 1999 a Salvadorean citizen, Raul Ernesto Cruz Leon, who Posada admitted was a mercenary working for him, was sentenced to death by the Cuban authorities after admitting to carrying out the attacks. The sentence was commuted to 30 years in prison in 2010. Posada lives as a free man in Miami.
2. In English in the original.
3. Tamal: a corn dish, where the corn is mashed and moulded into the shape of a cigarette packet.

The Trinity of Havana

Laidi Fernández de Juan

MARIA E NEVER KNEW anyone to quit smoking without claiming that they'd been on three packs a day until just the day before. Nor did she know anyone to have their appendix removed without saying the surgeon claimed that if they'd arrived three minutes later, it would have burst and caused fatal peritonitis. Similarly, she had never heard a single story about red tape genuinely being reduced in her country, even though the programme of 'de-bureaucratisation' was announced with great fanfare.

'*Something* had to be true,' she told herself, 'some mechanism had to be weakening the chains.'

This was the only explanation she could think of for why the newspapers kept talking about the willingness of the state to reduce formalities in the legal apparatus, even though Maria E had never seen a single, concrete example of it. This was why, after three years of procrastination on her part – not unlike the three packs of cigarettes and the three critical minutes between life and death – she resolved to contribute to the regulation of the city by registering, as legal property, the house in which three generations of her family had been living, ever since the year she was born.

'Three things Peru doesn't have, but Havana does: El Morro, La Cabaña, and a lover like you,' the residents of Havana used to say when they were kids, happy to live without an identity card or a mobile phone, let alone property. At that age, no one seemed to worry about material things. The enlightenment of poverty made everyone part of the same family, which in turn made the major transitions in life, from one stage to another, all the more bearable, being free of needing to rush from office to office trying to authenticate the status of 'owner'. As Maria E still had the unfinished business of 'House Registration' to see to, she took advantage of her early, voluntary retirement, and dedicated herself to the task – just at that moment when rumours started circulating through the streets of Havana that citizens would be relieved of this unforgiving and (as the practice showed) outdated legal process.

Three documents were needed to start the endlessly postponed marathon of recording the fact that her family was the owner of the Havana building where her kids had been born and learned to walk, and where she herself had opened her eyes for only the second time, on returning from the clinic where her mother had given birth to her, in this city they once called 'Courtesan of the Sun'.[1] A yellow certificate awarded to her grandmother – now deceased – congratulating her on being the owner of the house, was the first of the three essential papers. An application to confirm such ownership, made three years earlier, came second in line of importance. And finally, a notary's witnessing of her signature – granting her authority to deal with all things pertaining to registration, legalisation, authentication, and whatever other convolutions might come her way – conferred on Maria E the necessary legal power to face, with joy and enthusiasm, these apparently streamlined procedures.

According to the information she was given, her first task was to commission a plan of the house from a specialist experienced in such matters, outlining the house's perimeter and the property boundaries. This first step wasn't hugely inconvenient, it had to be said. Even though the damn office where you could wait for an appointment with one of these specialists – known as 'Community Architects' – didn't have any seats, it was still a nice place to wait. The grass outside where hopeful applicants could sit wasn't too itchy, the air wasn't unbearably humid and the dog shit was easily avoided. Although one of several signs on the door announced that contracts must be signed at 9am sharp, as is natural in Havana, nobody turns up before 10. This makes for some pleasant 'Vedadenese' conversation among the applicants ('El Vedado' being Maria E's neighbourhood), so that when people finally get served, no one is too surprised by the details that get shouted between the architect and his poor client – for what looks like the lobby to the office is actually the only place you can explain to anyone what is needed. The presence of everything outside of the lobby – the lawn, the front door covered in information posters, the staircase leading upwards, and the tiny room beyond – all seem superfluous to it. This was more an impersonation of an office than an actual one. But who cares about such details in Havana, let alone in El Vedado?

Maria E was eventually seen by an architect the same age as her son. A very friendly guy; confronted by her surprise at the lack of privacy (at the start of the procedure she was astonished, and showed it), he led her away by the hand and they resumed the meeting in a closet next to the door that served as an information wall. Suppressing her tendency for claustrophobia, Maria E found the courage to express her determination to legalise the only space she'd known as 'home' since she was born in El Vedado – that once aristocratic neighbourhood now showing all the signs of falling into ruin. Mercifully, this charming little boy, once he had taken off his barely noticeable earphones, explained the various steps she needed to take next. Going to the offices of UMIV would be her first step and then, after he had drawn up a plan of the house, she would need to register it at the Land Registry office, once any mistakes had been first corrected at a public notary's office. In other words, three more steps to go.

Not one for asking lots of questions, Maria E wrote everything down in a notebook she had already labelled 'Procedures' and, immediately after the meeting, brimming with energy, headed to what they call UMIV, the *Unidad Municipal de Inversiones de la Vivienda*,[2] several blocks away. Its whereabouts had been explained to her by a man who'd been her companion on the grass, among the dog shit, earlier that morning. Around mid-afternoon, having waited over three hours sitting on a stair that sagged rather comfortably in the middle, she was attended by a UMIV lady the age of her mother, who was kind enough to explain to her that her job was to confirm the number of each house. Despite the fact that our protagonist presented the lady with papers proving her Vedado house number had been set into the doorframe *before* the famous cyclone of 1926, the woman insisted she needed at least one more month to verify this, because in order to ensure this number was the correct one (which needed to be done *before* the architect could draw up *his* map with perimeter and boundaries included), she would need to draw up a different map first – of the block surrounding her house. In other words, she would have to visit the whole of El Vedado, draw a schemata of the house's surroundings, measure whatever was measurable from the asphalt of the street to the front door, and then and only then, determine that indeed the number provided was the correct one. Or not.

Six weeks later the same woman, the age of her mother, asked Maria E to return to the office that she shared – as is the tradition in Havana, even more so in El Vedado – with other UMIV officials. Little to her surprise (her astonishment was fading fast by this point), the woman informed her that, even though her house number was indeed correct, from then on, they would have to add a letter to the end of the number. In their case, the capital A. The lady smiled as she listened to Maria's objection that there was no B nor C near her house, so it didn't make sense to add an A. She smiled at our heroine, and replied enigmatically, 'One day you'll understand.'

Forty-six days after the initial submission, Maria E went back to the architects' office – the one with the grass – appropriately dressed for the picnic-like wait she knew to expect. She chatted with the others waiting there, just as friendly and laid-back as those she met the first time round: indeed, she thought some faces were, if quite not known to her, at least familiar. When her neighbourhood's kid-architect arrived, around 10am, he received her in the same closet, and promised to pay a visit to her house soon, and put the earphones he had taken off while she was talking back on. Our protagonist failed to realise that 'soon', for a government official, didn't mean anything less than three months. This had in fact been explained to her by a lady, same age as herself, who'd become her companion on this second picnic trip, while waiting among the dog shit for the noticeboard door to open, though she hadn't paid much attention to her at the time.

Maria E felt very lucky when the kid-architect visited before three months had even passed. Fortunately, the boy didn't notice the absence of the letter A at the end of the house number. He measured up, surveyed, and determined the limits, boundaries and the adjacent spaces divided up by the neighbours, then happily left. 'I'll call you when you can come and pick up the map,' he said. 'Someday soon you'll understand.'

Almost 23 months after her first foray into the Cuban de-bureaucratised process, Maria E made her way to the 'lawn' without being invited. This time she shared the place with five other applicants, among them a young maths student. There was enough time, while they waited, for him to explain the pain he'd suffered over three long years spent waiting between papers, offices, notaries and corrections. At last, around midday, an official emerged from one of the doors, whose posters announced new legal regulations (one in particular Maria E found very funny: *Each client must strictly refer only to HIS community architect, not to any other*) to inform them that, due to unforeseeable circumstances, no one could be seen before 3pm. The applicants were glad to hear the news (by this point the delays had gone beyond being annoying, and had actually become entertaining), because the mathematician had had the brilliant idea of suggesting that, while they waited among the dog shit, they undertake a mental exercise: try to guess which of the six of them would be the first to leave with his or her problem solved – though they hadn't fully appreciated his point that this puzzle might be therapeutic.

To carry out the game, the young mathematician explained to them the theorems and principles of probability, which was not only extremely instructive but also managed to render the waiting rather pleasant. After stating his admiration for some Russian called Andréi Nikoláyevich Kolmogórov (a Siberian genius of probability theory, apparently) he talked to them about the Pigeonhole Principle.

As they were waiting in a place previously used as a toilet by Vedado's dogs, the student thought the reference to pigeons would be appropriate. According to the Principle, explained passionately by the maths pigeon, if there are more pigeons than coops, at least one of the coops would need to host at least two pigeons at any one time. Maria E admitted, with great immodesty, that of the five people sitting around the student, she was the only one to understand that if n (number of pigeons) is bigger than m (coops), then clearly the Principle holds. The bewilderment shown by the rest of the group prompted the boy into providing a new example. That's when he seemed to hit the mark. A certain Ramsey,[3] in 1928 (no one knew if that was the year he was born or the year he elaborated his great theorem, called the 'Theorem of Friends and Strangers') stated that in any meeting of six people, either three of them know each other or three of them don't know each other.

Once the condition was met by which nobody had met any of the others face-to-face before and, the real probability was added to this, that at least one of them would solve their problem that very afternoon, the applicants' spirits rose to unexpected heights. With one exception: an old philosophy professor who said he didn't want to take part in the game, as he believed he was witnessing a dangerous slide towards a doctrine known as Probabilism, according to which every action depends on opinions which are never totally false nor totally true.

Faced with such an accusation, and uncertain as to whether this would benefit or harm them, the gathered *Vedadenese* stayed silent and looked to the young university student, who had immediately stopped talking. An obese woman took a plaster statue of Saint Barbara out of her bag; a teenager spat on the ground and murmured something unrepeatable about older generations; while the only representative of the new business class populating the country – a well-built fifty-something who hadn't stopped lighting Marlboros all day – produced a bottle of Chivas Regal from his bag and took a long glug. Maria E, meanwhile, took advantage of this general astonishment to write in her 'Procedures' notebook the following, intending to look at it later:

Probably there is some order at work in the state offices, similar to that found in the pigeonholes, whose essence we can't fully grasp for the simple fact that we ignore how probabilistic our condition is and live under the false assumption that we are either totally right or totally wrong in our decisions. It's neither one thing nor the other, or in fact it's both.

It was three in the afternoon when three officials finally opened the office door. By this point, only three of the applicants remained on the grass. Three minutes multiplied by three officials, repeating, on three different occasions, that they could enter, with the people on the grass, for the same number of times, refusing the invitation because they were too engrossed in trying to solve an algebraic problem – a much more entertaining activity than asking for papers that would never appear. Night fell on Maria E and the mathematician, wrapping up the Blessed Saint Barbara that the obese woman had asked them, three minutes after three, to take care of while she went off for a minute to complain to the office of the local television news programme, known as 'Your Vedado, Happy and Nice'.

'Tell me again, slowly this time, what the Russian said,' Maria E begged this disciple of Pythagoras.

As the third neighbourhood dog came out to shit on the grass, the aspiring mathematician concluded his paper, and only then did she understood how extremely lucky it was to be living in a de-bureaucratised city. If it hadn't been for his explanation, she would have remained lost in the darkness of a dreadful limbo, forever ignorant of the importance of binomial inclusion–exclusion, the Multiplication Principle, and how crucial it is to learn the different ways to perform combinations. 'I'm giving up this application, I surrender,' she told the student. 'But I am thankful of the fact that I know Havana has three things that Peru doesn't have: El Vedado, my home and a scientist like you. Or vice versa, who cares!'

'What about the papers registering your property?' asked the student. 'Are you not going to ask for them back?'

'Oh, my child,' Maria E replied, 'I've turned half-probabilist myself. Even though it's not all true or all false, my home is mine because Havana is mine. Because El Vedado is mine. And because, with or without papers, I can't deny the essential, inherent and immutable condition that these are the three truly important things: the trinity of Havana.'

'And what are they?' enquired the boy.

'Ah...,' she said. 'Some day you'll understand. You know a lot about numbers and theorems, but you lack an understanding of pain, of wounds. How can I put it? You haven't yet found out what an esoteric shrew Havana is. Come, I'll get you a coffee and on the way I'll tell you more.'

Thus they were seen passing through El Vedado: the fifty-something Marie E and a boy, who looked just as you'd expect a student of the mathematical sciences to look, strolling down the cracked streets – those dirty, deserted, ancient and incomparable streets – in a city they couldn't abandon, even though no one would ever give them a property title or, for that matter, anything else.

Notes

1. Credited to Jorge Mañach (1898-1961); a Cuban journalist, philosopher, essayist and biographer of José Martí.

2. The Local Housing Investment Office

3. Frank P. Ramsey, 1903-1930; British mathematician and friend of Ludwig Wittgenstein (who he also translated) at Cambridge University. Following his 1928 paper 'On a problem of formal logic' one of the theorems of combinatorial mathematics was named after him (Ramsey's theorem).

My Night

Eduardo Angel Santiesteban

ONLY 11PM AND ALREADY the patrol has made its first arrests.
I'm sure there's a connection. Tonight, their pockets will be
filled in direct proportion to how full their cells become, I'll
bet you. I'm sat at the corner of Malecón and Paseo, in front
of the Fuente de la Juventud,[1] – although I'm not sure we're
the kind of 'juventud' they had in mind. I'm with Toni, one of
my best friends. This is our graduation day so we're celebrating
with a bottle of vodka that's already nearing the bottom.

A wino shuffles towards us. He's talking to himself and that
makes him the butt of our jokes: this is our future, we say, maybe
even in an hour's time. Then I realise, as far as I know, I'm as far
gone as he is, so I decide to go easy on the drink, at least for the
time being. Three metres away the man stumbles and falls and
everyone laughs. I get up to help him but my friend grabs my
arm to stop me. I free myself and help the man up. I ask him if
he's hurt, and he says no, swings his arm across my shoulder,
lowers his head and throws up all over my shoes. I look up at the
sky and take a deep breath, all the time hearing the others
laughing at me. I should have listened to Toni, I reflect, even
though I know he didn't do it deliberately. I suggest to him
gently that he take a walk and get some air, imploring also that,
if he is going to throw up again, he doesn't do it on me.

I return to my friend, sporting my best carefree expression.
Sitting down, I take another swig and light the last cigarette. Toni
gets up and goes to buy another pack. Turning my back to the

street I start to stare out at the sea, when suddenly someone touches my shoulder: I turn and find myself staring at a petite little girl with a rockin' body and a gorgeous face. She asks for a light; I get my lighter out, but instead she takes the cigarette out of my mouth. Who knows who she's going out with; it doesn't matter. When she has lit hers with mine she hands my cigarette back and sits down beside me. The ice is broken with a question, cool and disinterested: 'Have you got a girlfriend?'

'No,' I answer.

'I liked how you dealt with the wino,' she says. 'Did you do that to impress me?

'No. That's just the way I was brought up,' I shrug. 'What's your name?'

But instead of answering she asks if I've ever spent a night with someone without knowing a thing about them.

'Yes, but not in the way you mean, not like this. It was with people I never wanted to see again.' Almost before I could finish the sentence she kisses me.

'This is what I'm offering you,' she says, 'to spend the night without knowing a single thing about me.'

'Nor you knowing anything about me?' I ask her.

'Well, it's essential if we are to see each other again,' she says.

'And what do I call you in the meantime?'

'You can call me Luna.'

As the night progresses, somewhere in between endless kisses and laughter, she does indeed ask me about myself. The sea begins to turn angry and its spray splashes over us, so we decide to take a walk. We cross the street and head up Calle G, then find somewhere to sit and chat on Calle 25. Around 2.30am she tells me she has to go. Desperate to know more about her, I ask if she'll at least let me walk her home. She agrees and, having been so convinced she'd say no, I'm amazed that such a simple thing could produce so much childish delight. As usual, we wait an age at the bus stop. It's 3.30am when the P9 finally arrives, stopping, unusually, right in front of us. *This must be my night,* I think. We sit at the back. As the *guagua*[2] is almost empty, with only a few passengers up at the front, I light a cigarette. It's cold, so I lend her my coat, and she leans over and hugs me. From this moment on, I realise something special is growing deep in my chest and I can't explain it. As we approach her stop she gives the coat back with a passionate kiss that leaves a sad smile on my face.

'Am I getting off with you?'

'No, our night ends here.'

And before she alights I ask her what feels like the most important question of my life: 'Will I see you again?'

'Maybe,' she answers.

She steps off and the driver closes the door to set off again. I will never be able understand why I just carry on sitting there. She stares at the *guagua* as it departs, and I notice that right behind her there's a window in which mannequins stand elegantly attired in evening dresses. If it was up to me, I think, the next time we meet she would be wearing one of those.

I get off at the next stop and cross the street to the taxi rank. After a thirty minute wait, I climb into an *almendron,*[3] unable to stop thinking about her, the wondrous night we'd just had, and when we might see each other again. Butterflies fluttered, as they say in the movies. *Will we meet tomorrow? I will just have to wait and see.*

When I get home I head straight to my mum's room to fetch the key to mine. She keeps it in there when I'm out – her way of knowing the time I get back each night. My response is to fish it out without waking her. Most nights I pull it off, and tonight I'm opening my bedroom door knowing she hasn't moved a millimetre. I undress and get into bed.

I hear my name. Without opening my eyes I know it's my mother, and she's making breakfast. I hate being woken up like this, but she insists I cannot go so many hours without eating.

As I digest the food, I contemplate the previous night and its wonderful encounter. It also dawns on me quite how late it was when I got in. Having finished eating, I place the tray on the bedside table, and switch the light off to go back to sleep.

'You not getting up today?' she asks.

'Why?'

'You've been asleep for fifteen hours.'

'Mum, I was up very late last night,' I counter, thus giving away everything I'd tried to hide.

'No, last night you fell asleep waiting for the water to heat up,' she says, and only when she looks at my face does she realise nothing she is saying computes.

'OK, look...' she goes to the kitchen and returns with a burnt and blackened saucepan - the one we use for heating water for the bath.

'Last night, it burnt because you fell asleep.'

I'm surprised by this but I don't feel like being interrogated any more.

My mother leaves and closes the door behind her.

As I recollect the night before, various pieces fit together. That said, my mum's story is a good one also. Toni is the only one who will settle things, I realise, and reach for the phone. His mother answers and tells me he's out playing football at the Martí.[4]

I get dressed and head out. When I reach the sports ground I see Toni running around on the field. I lean on a wall, waiting for him to finish, all the time trying to prepare myself psychologically for the possibility that he might confirm my mother's story. The game ends and he jogs over to greet me. He asks if I've put my name down on the list to play already. I tell him I don't feel like it.

'So, why did you come?'

'To talk to you.'

'About what?' he asks, a little distracted.

'About last night.'

'What about it?' Finally he's intrigued.

'What happened to me?'

He assures me that nothing happened: I didn't go out. He waited for me, but I never arrived.

I fail to comprehend. Both my mother and Toni seem to be confirming a hypothesis, according to which I never went out last night. My heart refuses to believe this. I know for certain I met that girl. I walk home. When I arrive I go to the kitchen where I inspect the saucepan we use for heating water: no trace of burning. I shout out my mother to ask if she's just bought a new saucepan.

'No, why?'

'The saucepan was burnt this morning and now it isn't.'

'I don't know what you're talking about,' she replies.

'Are you saying the saucepan was never burned because I feel asleep?'

'Of course not,' she assures me. 'Why would you want the pot to get burned?'

'Nothing, that's my business.'

I storm off and lock myself in my bedroom. I can't understand what's going on. All I know is *she* exists and that's the best thing that could have happened to me.

A few minutes later I'm out of my room and getting ready to hit the town. My mother asks what bug has just bitten me but I don't answer. I'm in a hurry. I need to find her as soon as possible, and tell her she's become the most important thing in my life. My anxiety mounts as I wait for the *guagua* to take me to her neighbourhood; it cannot arrive soon enough. Without thinking, I stick out my hand and hail a cab.

I say nothing to the driver, except to give him the exact address. Despite the car's obvious speed, to me it feels like we're riding on the back of a tortoise. In half an hour, I'm at the corner where I saw her for the last time. My plan is to retrace the footsteps I watched her take from the back seat of the *guagua*, maybe even to trace her scent, make out her footprints, whatever is needed to find her house, so I can hold her. I see the shop window long before I get to it and I'm surprised not to see evening dresses. Instead there are umbrellas on display. As I walk up to it, I realise there's a man looking through the window at them. I ask him if the place was a clothes shop before, one that sold evening dresses. The man looks calmly at me, then looks at the window: 'Not since I was a child, this place has always been an umbrella shop.' He shows me the one hanging from his arm, then throws it in the air, catches it, and hits me on the leg with it.

The pain in my leg forces me to wake up; it's numb from me sleeping on it awkwardly. Dawn is breaking. My friend has left without a word. I look down at my shoes still stained with the wino's vomit. *That son of a bitch*, I think, *forcing me to be a good Samaritan. I should've listened to Toni.* I manage to stretch my legs and straighten my back, although it causes a new pain, this time running down my spine. I stagger to my feet and start looking for a *guagua*.

Somebody shouts at me and waves his hands. I have the worst hangover, and can't process what he's saying, but when he gets closer I realise it's Toni.

'What's up with you?' he asks mockingly.

If he were in my place, as sick as I feel, he wouldn't be laughing.

I say hi and tell him I'm going home. Before I leave he asks me if my night had ended successfully, with the olive-skinned girl of the Malecón.

He keeps talking, but I don't hear him, any more.

Notes

1. The *Fuente de la Juventud* -- Fountain of Youth — constructed in August 1978 for the 11th Festival of Youth and Students held in Havana.

2. Cuban word for a very particular kind of bus.

3. Cuban name for the old 1950's American cars.

4. Martí - Parque José Martí, located near the Malecón and built during the 1940s, is a sports and recreational space, redeveloped after the revolution, but currently in a dilapidated state.

An 'Ali Khan Day'

Francisco López Sacha

ALI KHAN'S DAYS WERE always glorious. He would rise early, at the break of dawn, and, wrapped in an embroidered gown, look out through the glass wall of one of his villas. While the sun was still rising – through the fog of London, over the distant dunes around Cairo, or through the almond and orange trees of Seville – he would ask for tea to be brought. Quietly he would sip the infusion, as well-brewed as it was aromatic, in the golden light, and set about his first assignment. Afterwards, he would take a bath – European style, with lukewarm water, seated in a walnut tub; or American style, invigoratingly hot in a bath fitted with immaculate white handles; or Slavic style, standing and whipping his back with a sheaf of watercress; or Oriental style, with scented water, surrounded by incense burners – and then emerge, soaking wet, wrapped in a plush robe, his face flushed, his body refreshed, still firm save for a few small ripples of fat around the belly, to step out onto soft rugs if he were in New York, onto marble tiles if he were in Naples, or onto a mat, if he were in Rabat, Algiers or Islamabad. His image stared back at him from the mirror, as the last trickle of water ran dry. He had thin, chestnut hair, a wide round face, and a sincere and gentle smile. He would then comb his hair, shave, finish his ablutions and, always looking to the west, he would pray.

Later, around mid-morning, he would converse with one of his guests – an English financier, a Jordanian or North

African prince, or one of his close friends – about his stable of thoroughbred horses, oil prices on the Stock Exchange, the weather, or his latest conquest (Eastern women didn't count, nor did Turkish, Armenian, Egyptian, or Syrian), then suddenly his eyes would light up – they would be dark, very dark until that point – and he would raise his voice to ask: 'What if we had lunch in Paris?' 'Maybe we should lunch in Rome?' 'How about an evening in Istanbul?' He would order his car, or rather one of his cars (Rolls Royce, Ferrari, Alfa Romeo), and drive to the nearest hangar – one with its own private runway - where a helpful pilot and navigator would lead him to the aircraft, and four or five hours later... there he was: at Maxim's, or La Coupole or on the terrace of his country house in Sardinia overlooking a rocky costal landscape, asking to be served a burgundy or a Napoleon brandy.

Each of Ali Khan's days were different, more than that, they were unique. The weightlessness of mornings would dissolve into words exchanged between sips of tea, across a service of porcelain crockery from Sèvres, German silverware, and Peruvian cup holders, wafted through the smoke of Monterrey or H. Upmann cigars, from the farms of Robaina,[1] interrupted only by the occasional ring of a bell, calling for ginger and saffron cakes, like the ones the pharaohs would eat on their papyrus boats. The morning would drift on like this until eleven o'clock, when the last rain on the pavements of Kensington Road would evaporate in the sun. 'What do you think,' he would say, 'about having dinner in Mónaco?' 'How about grilled sardines in Portobello? Shall we say a Chianti in Liguria?' Then he would laugh heartily, with every fibre of his plump frame, baring his teeth and gums, and outstretching his hands to his interlocutor, the ring finger of one hand glinting murkily with an ancient, bronze band once worn by Cyrus the Great, king of kings.

Each of Ali Khan's days – uninterrupted by strikes, riots, or regime changes – was wondrous, authentic, distinct. Dinner in Paris under chandeliers (seafood starters, a sorbet soon after to cleanse the palate). Breakfast in Sorrento, in the shade of a beachfront awning. A short regatta across the Tyrrhenian at sunset, with the last golden rays warming his shoulders. A Maria Callas concert in Milan – her soprano voice rebounding off the ceiling and horseshoe auditorium of the Scala, only to then burst and envelop each and every one: a voice, without a hint of *rubato*, trailing off to mingle with the rapturous applause as it reached the red, velvet chairs of the stalls, only to climb again, and reverberate through the royal boxes, where dozens of elegant people, now on their feet, clapped their hands. A fleeting visit to Hollywood, a furtive encounter with Rita Hayworth on the set of *The Lady from Shanghai*. And so on...

Incomparable days, days that would never be repeated: in Lisbon, in Tangiers, in Palermo. A single extended rotation of the Earth would find him, one day, under a tent at the court of King Farouk; the next evening at the Metropolitan Opera House in the company of Jill Saint John; in Porto, the day after, in Madrid the morning after that; or else in his immense suite of offices with his father, the Aga Khan, following a spin in the Maserati at 180kmh. Ali Khan, the crown prince, in his royal box, with that captivating voice in a single-button tuxedo. Ali Khan, standing in front of an enormous wedding cake celebrating his engagement to Rita Hayworth, captured in the society pages of *The Bohemia*, as the Earth continued rotating on its axis. A cake with eight tiers and 40 layers, immaculately white, decorated with intricate scrolls and lace meringues, layers of pure flavour blended together with a secret stuffing of semolina, date cream, almond liqueur, cocoa, tropical fruit and hashish. All this with two wax models of the couple planted on the summit.

Day dawned brightly on the crest of Havana's Malecón. It looked like an 'Ali Khan day', only designed by me. Or rather, designed by Carla, who was now serving me breakfast in bed on a silver tray – Carla, who had slipped through the doorway with a delicate swing of her bony shoulders, hidden under a silk robe, her long legs and bare feet undulating gently as she stepped across the carpet. A service of white porcelain cups preceded her, one steaming with tea, the other with chocolate, alongside a multicoloured glass filled with pineapple juice, some recently-baked cakes, toast, and a raspberry jam tart, exactly as I'd asked for them.

Carla approached me very sweetly, placed the tray on my chest and threw back her thick blonde hair – hair that smelled of Pantene, slightly shaven at the neck, straight on the sides – brushing my face with it as she did so, then looked at me sadly with eyes so clear and green with the slightest trace of brown. Her thick-lipped smile, still smudged with the remains of last night's lipstick, hinted at the paler, natural pink beneath. Last night's smell also clung to her robe, a subtle scent of her sweat, mixed with the more elusive fragrance of lotion, rum, maraschino, and something stronger permeating from down below, the dark cluster of hair, which, like her armpits, she hadn't shaved. 'Just to get you excited, my love,' she'd said once in the innocent accent of a girl from Cáceres. 'Look,' she said suddenly, 'I've already said: today we do whatever you want, and when the day is over I have a surprise for you.'

'Give it to me now,' I replied, feeling an intense tingling beneath the sheet making me rise to the day.

I drank the juice – nothing more – and put the tray down on the floor, sliding it almost entirely under the bed, then turned back towards her, where she was waiting for me, her legs slightly parted, the belt of her robe undone. I flipped her roughly onto her back and stroked the dark hair below –

always a surprise for such a blonde woman. Then I began stroking her thighs, from bottom to top. I couldn't help myself. I climbed on top of her, and rubbed myself against her for as long as I could stand it before finally penetrating her. (Actually, maybe I should confess: I did all this rather hastily, in reality, grunting and grinding before shoving it in.) But if I confessed this, I wouldn't be able to describe the sunlight, or the beauty of the morning, or compare myself, in dreams, with the chronicles of that golden age and those delicate stories of the gallant Ali Khan, nor could I picture myself in one of those old Hollywood movies, riding a cherry-coloured convertible down Sunset Boulevard, with an actress beside me letting her blonde hair blow in the wind as she purses her deep, purple lips.

Just like in that dream, the daylight now refracted through the blinds as Carla buried her head – which sometimes looked like that of a teenager – into the pillow. She tightened her lips and closed her eyes, arching her back to each new thrust. She whimpered and the silk robe, slipping from side to side, made a contrast between its smooth, wine-coloured fabric and her white skin, which seemed to bristle each time I moved in and out, while opening the other untouchable orifice with my thumb and forefinger, as if threateningly. This was a game I'd learned to play with Carla on a previous adventure – in a room trespassed into at noon: Tany's room in fact, on the corner of Zanja and Manrique,[2] after a date with a large quantity of rum. Carla knew what I liked and offered this pleasure up to me despite herself, and if I was able to time it right, I'd take it. Not that she would deny me; she would simply offer it to me, then take it away, teasing. At first, she would open herself wide and cling to me and from that position she would slide backward and forward, making me come instantly. And then she would tease me, pretending that she wanted to please me the other way, knowing I was spent. It was a game of chance which I would always lose, maybe because I got too excited. Today, though, I wanted to enjoy it for real, to violate that sweet opening, clenching me hard with its dry, fiery heat, till I was breathless.

In this version of the game Carla's body clung to mine but I managed to push it away. Often she was too strong for me, but this time I manage to wriggle out, holding her by the waist, and freezing all my other muscles so as not to come. I was engulfed by the heat and broke into a sweat, while beneath me she whispered coarse words in a language that seemed foreign to me. She had to first believe that I was about to come – from my tense, sudden movements – then I pulled out and, before she could react or say no, I plunged deep into her ass, and that delicious tight hole gave way, gripping tightly at first and then softening obediently, allowing me to fit inside her. Then, in full command of her body, I heard a deep sigh slip from her lips, accompanied by a shudder, as the thickest part of me forced its way deep in.

'Thank you for this surprise, honey.'

After we'd showered – American style, piping hot, in a cloud of vapour – and with our bodies clean, rested and fed by a hearty breakfast, Carla sat naked on the footstool in front of the dresser, applying creams to her still-wet body, an enormous mirror allowing me to observe her, both front and back, all the way down to the tangle of her pubic hair, and the soft perfect pink below. At times she shook her head, sending a fine shower of moisture back and forth with her hair, which fell in disarray. Perched on the edge of the bed, I watched as she offered me her latest gift: a pair of blue Flexi moccasins, then returned to touching her breasts and tilting her neck, looking at her nipples quizzically, or flexing her torso to touch her feet, her right leg propped up on the ottoman, or bringing her face close to the mirror to put her make-up on – mouth slightly open and even her teeth and the tip of her tongue poised, as if dawn had only just broken.

If I were not in love with Tany, and her gentle, whore-like ways, her hard body, her habit of peeing shamelessly in front of me, and above all, the tone of her voice, I could fully surrender to Carla: to the hedonistic and solitary pleasure of passing from one week (or fortnight) to the next, free from all pressures, living only on the stash of reddies she slipped me, as pocket money, or skillfully tucked into the back pocket of my jeans, patting me down as she did so, whether out on the street or in this room, with its sea view, rented by her openly at first, then in secret, bribing both the doorman and the elevator operator – a carpeted suite on the ninth floor of the Hotel Riviera,[3] from which you could see the sunrise in all its splendour: cobalt blue, with a hint of orange, distant, bright and blinding.

But I was missing Tany – the nights she spent with me, the smell of her sweat, her quickening breath, her dark straightened hair, totally artificial, which I could grab hold of and pull, her laughter, the crude words of a coarse Havana girl, her way of giving herself to me immediately, whenever I wanted, in the confined space of the kitchen or the toilet, and her way of saying, in the latter space, crouched over, and with no little chutzpah, as she fixed her eyes on mine and dried herself with toilet paper: 'OK, but just a quickie.'

But whenever I was living that life, I quickly began to miss this other one, even after a week: that life without pressure or haste, with money on tap; the easy life that Tany could not give me.

'Rolen, honey...' Carla's voice, as if dubbed in Spanish, reflected off the mirror and echoed unpleasantly through the empty space of the suite. 'Shall we take that boat ride, this morning?' She was referring to an old-fashioned ship reconstructed from priceless timbers that we'd seen anchored at Muelle de Luz the night before, with all its rigging, ropes and sails. A galleon, that only accepted one currency onboard – dollars – that swelled its sails each morning and looked like nothing more than a fancy toy as it passed in front of the Malecón. A galleon for corsairs and pirates, as dreamt up by the Town Historian.

This was Carla's second trip to the island and yet still she knew nothing of our dreams, our quixotic vision of the world, not even our childish idea of what success meant. Neither was she aware of our insatiable preoccupation with pleasure. More, always more, was our motto. Carla, however, didn't imitate us, didn't make fun of us, nor did she know how to pronounce *nagüe, naguito*,[4] even if she frequently and hilariously dropped them into conversation.

It was her second trip to Cuba but the first in which I'd decided to tell her, because I could no longer bear the thought of lying (and because Carla had seen me with Tany, near the Barrio Chino, the night before renting the Riviera suite). I decided to tell her, with a glass of whisky in front of me filled to the brim, that I wasn't really asking for much, that I just wanted to enjoy the moment and have a good time, and, at the same time, of course, stay with Tany. I asked her this out of the blue – not wanting her to throw a tantrum, out of jealousy or from being offended as a woman. At this Carla, who did not know Tany, but who had seen her from a distance, hugged me, and accepted the deal. From then on, the days would be for her, the nights for Tany – a deal I tried to soften by granting her each sunrise, something intimate and private, in truth something most important to me.

We were in the Mina de Oro, at one of the tables on Calle Obispo, being deafened by a trio of awful *guaracheros*[5], when Carla, with a half-full glass of her favourite Havana Club in front of her, suddenly forced a smile, and accepted the cruel truth. But on one condition – so long as it didn't adversely affect me – that I would introduce Tany to her that very evening, and invite her to the Torre de Marfil.[6] I lowered my head, nodding (already sorry that I had been so candid). Then I decided to smoke one last menthol, from Carla's pack of Merrits, and stare through the smoke into the Plaza de las Armas, the sun shimmering on the wooden cobblestones, and at the lonely shelves of the antique bookcases, filled with maps, old magazines and books for the tourists, indeed where my own stand, at the very beginning of Calle O'Reilly, stood deserted.

I delivered on my commitment by phone and Tany arrived, wearing a flowery evening dress, her lips full and red, looking somehow defiant and timid at the same time. Carla stared into her eyes, examining her face, her body, her bronze skin, no doubt comparing her to herself, then began chatting comfortably, even ordering things for her. She smiled openly, as if this was her friend, not my lover, talking about her life in Cáceres and her holidays on the Costa Brava, about her taste for expensive clothes and Nina Ricci perfumes, about the oysters soaked in Australian beer that she could only get in the Fulton Market. They even smiled at each other, a wide open smile, and, two glasses of wine later, with a slight tremor to her voice, Tany asked her tentatively how she could afford this high life.

They went to the bathroom together, I guess to fix their make-up, and when they returned they seemed ecstatic. I was amazed, if perplexed to see them getting on so well, and, before we left, Carla even presented Tany with a golden bracelet inlaid with ivory that she'd bought at Tiffany's last summer. 'Take it, gorgeous; it's yours,' she said. And of course, that very night, Carla rewarded me for my honesty, promising me yet another 'Ali Khan Day'.

At 10am we took a taxi from the entrance to the Hotel Riviera down to the Muelle de Luz, feeling fresh and rejuvenated. We sat ourselves on the foredeck of the galleon, facing the wide expanse of the bay, just as she unfurled her sails and slowly began navigating through the dense, oily water. The customs building was to our left, while in front stood the stone wall of the Cabaña fortress. As we passed the Morro castle, the sea began to settle into a dark blue, and Carla ordered a whisky with ice for me and a Havana Club for herself. The breeze beat against my face; now that the galleon was entering into deeper and rougher waters, and facing starboard, into the wind, I could see the distant, whitewashed porches of the limestone houses lining the coast, their tiny cars parked out front, and even the moving silhouettes of fishermen along the sea wall. Our lives seemed to shrink as the galleon sailed away from the coast until only the tallest buildings of Vedado peeked out through the shroud of violet light. Ali Khan had a perfect life, but not this one, not mine. Although I envied his days, his money, I didn't care about racehorses, nor the Middle East, nor the Earth, which I do not feel rotate on its axis the way he did. I care only about the sky, pleasant company, the stormy blue sea, and this life I lead right now, *this one,* going nowhere in particular. Carla beside me. Tany, where she'll always be. Havana beneath my feet, maybe without the stench of certain streets, ideally, and minus the shithole where I live, take away the smell of old parchment in the shop where I buy bread, and the hours I spend with chapped lips at that spot in the Plaza de Armas, hawking the dubious merchandise that is used books, rebound by yours truly: slim volumes or thick hardbacks, dusty, worn out, their grey *bodoni* typeface fading – for four dollars, five dollars, ten – and magazines: *Cuba at Hand, Cuban Counterpoint,* style mags, *Bohemia, El Monte, Cecilia Valdés, Sóngoro Cosongo, La Fijeza, The Kingdom of this World, A King in the Garden*; books that come and go, torn, mouldy, looted from ancient shelves, sometimes even public libraries... maybe without all of that;

66

but *here,* this *mare aperto*[7] haven where I am king, prince (even of this accursed life), standing on the deck of a golden galleon now approaching the bend of the Almendares River, with the first mansions of Miramar to our right, and the glare of the sun directly above. This moment now, sharing a second double whisky, with Carla's hair blowing in the breeze, clinging to her face so close to mine – the very wind flustered by her beauty – and the pair of us leaning together over the railing into that expanse of blue profaning the whiteness of clouds, the swaying and lapping of the waves, the billowing of the sails, and Carla enquiring shyly, hesitantly, timidly about Tany's situation: 'What does she do for a living? What's her occupation?... No, no reason, just asking.'

The galleon swung out beyond the bend of the river, helped along by the breeze coming off the land. I decided we should have lunch at El Aljibe: I was in the mood for a fine charcoal-grilled chicken with a stew of red beans.

From Avenida del Puerto, we took a taxi and I wound down the window to get a hot blast from the midday Havana sun. En route we watched as the decaying (soon to be non-existent) porticos of the houses along the Malecón passed by, the dirty, unpainted doorways, and the bicycle-taxis going in every direction – their drivers sweating over handlebars: dark-skinned men wearing black shirts with fat, old tourists lounging comfortably in the back, taking polaroids of each camel[8] to crawl up and down San Lazaro, from Maceo Park. The Malecón widened at 23rd Street, where La Roca brandished a Cuban flag from its highest balcony. Carla stared through the taxi window at the imposing mass of the Hotel Nacional, saying she needed a mental photograph of it. But nothing mattered to me. Not the people I could see strolling in single file down the side of the Interests Section[9], nor the low-rise houses half-eaten away by saltpetre, nor their rusty (soon to be non-existent) gates, nor the tinted windows of the

Casa de las Américas. Nothing mattered but this lazy drunkenness carrying me forward into the tunnel on Fifth Avenue, this freedom, basking in the shade of the evergreens and date palms on Calle 10, in an oasis that only turns completely green for a week, maybe fifteen days a year. Nothing mattered but being there with Carla, who paid for everything, and Tany, who offered me everything her body could, later in the lethargy of the night.

El Aljibe wasn't too hot, perhaps because of the insistent rustling of the breeze on its thatched roof, or the spacious lay-out of its rooms, or the Heineken beer, or the cold napkin that Carla kept patting my face with. Now I really felt on my throne, kissing her, caressing her hands, stroking her blonde, almost thoroughbred head – true, I didn't much care for horses, although, maybe, I could appreciate the funny noises mares made, in heat, whenever they were about to be mounted. Now I felt uplifted by the vertigo of the whisky, by the effervescence of the beer, as if ascending gently into my true kingdom (a worldly one for sure, but *this* kingdom, *this* paradise!), being greeted by the flesh of a charcoal-grilled chicken thigh and a bowl of thick stew – its aroma rising like the chorus of women praising the Almighty for the food and eating hungrily next to us – in this dollars-only world I had built for myself over the past year, or rather the world I had *been able* to build for myself.

We ate our fill, and had two more beers. Then Carla asked for a maraschino, her favourite liquor, at the bar outside.

Carla sipped her drink as I watched. Nearby, a sexy little whore with very smooth skin, large, dark eyes and high cheekbones, bare-shouldered, sunburned, wearing a tight top and denim shorts, was finishing her daiquiri. Carla looked her up and down and then stopped, looking her in the eye. They stared at length. When I looked over at her (something elusive about her reminded me of Tany), she lowered her gaze, uncomfortable. Then she got up and left.

The light became still, incandescent, and the breeze began to soften, making way for the siesta. I began to resent the smell of food, the sticky, greasy aroma emitting from the other rooms with their tables and awful chequered tablecloths. I suggested to her that we escape to Marina Hemingway, have a mojito, or something else, and watch the yachts pass through the canals at Barlovento. 'Whatever you say, my king,' Carla said, pouting her lips and forcing an abrupt smile.

Barlovento offered a brilliant panorama at three in the afternoon: a few yachts coming in or going out, each one leaving a wide trough in its wake. And, despite the heat, or rather the torpor that seemed to evaporate even the sea, its gardens, its two-storey houses, and the very moorings themselves all managed to preserve some of the relief of an oasis, under the harsh sunlight, in this exclusive, off-the-beaten-track location, where those tourists that weren't driving Audis walked in groups towards The Old Man and the Sea[10] and the docks. As much as I wanted to get going, and as much as Carla kept pointing towards the last houses carved out of stone, wanting to ask questions, my day was slipping hopelessly into that unbearable time that could only be alleviated by air conditioning. I ordered a mojito which I drank thirstily and then another; then a White Horse whisky which clouded my eyes so much I thought the day of this particular oriental prince had come to an end, a scheduled rest, even when Carla pinched me to wake me up, and let slip her spiteful question: 'Does this happen to you when you're with Tany?'

Actually, the whole thing was feeling like a bad idea (I knew yesterday's decision might backfire, and I should have expected her reproach). I needed to get back to the Riviera to take a nap and then get ready for the night ahead I had planned in Tany's bed. It was 4.30pm before I summoned the courage to start making hints about leaving, when I was almost overcome with fatigue, and could bear it no longer.

As we left, we embraced and started walking slowly together: I thought I heard an old song, 'Pretty Blue Eyes' by Steve Lawrence, coming from the end of the pier, or from a yacht moored in the distance. Curiously, it was in Spanish, a version by Dany Puga. I must have been mistaken, maybe it was all in my head, which was beginning to spin in the *panataxi*[11] from the scorching sun and the strange glare of the day gone by... The dizziness continued propelling my thoughts into the arms of Tany, in that bedroom on the corner of Zanja and Manrique, with its window thrown open in the middle of the suffocating night, stifled by the warm breeze of the fan, soaking me in sweat, as I held her so tightly, for fear of losing her, losing my sweet Tany, who was biting my neck and kissing me hard as she straddled my lap, naked, back arched, with her firm and powerful buttocks.

Carla woke me up when we reached the Riviera. She paid the bill and left the driver a more-than-generous tip which I had hoped to avoid. She begged me to go on up alone, she had to go to the ATM.

'Where?' I asked.

'The ATM.'

'Which one?'

'The one between Linea and A – the only one that takes my card,' she explained. 'I need to withdraw money for tonight, money to dance with NG La Banda in the Casa de la Musica in Miramar.'

'NG La Banda? Why?'

'You know, tonight...'

She gave me a kiss. I saw her walking away through the parking lot out front. I was hesitant to go up, a little crazy, unable to walk much further, my body ready to collapse, overcome with sleep, with the heat and the pinching of the new loafers I had put on without socks. I passed through Reception and waited quietly for the elevator boy to get me upstairs. Now my head hurt.

The sun had set already, gloriously, with its faint, golden pink and heavenly blue afterglow − a blend of colours impossible to describe. I ordered a beer from room service and a little crushed ice to alleviate my hangover.

I dozed on the wide bed, without undressing, waiting for Carla. A faint hum filled the air and the freshness of the ice-cold towel over my face worked its magic. I woke in the dark, startled and alone, failing to comprehend.

A cold sweat covered me. I groped across the suite in the darkness, hearing nothing but the dull squeak of my shoes, not knowing what to do. Turning on the light, I looked everywhere for clues: checked the nightstand, the dresser drawers, the desk, the hallway, then walked to the closet and went through the back pockets of Carla's Levis, a pair of Lees, her combat trousers. I made up the bed with a growing sense of anger, then found myself staring, annoyed, into the bathroom mirror, inspecting my bloodshot eyes that seemed slightly frightened by the fact that the yellow hands of my Quantum Black watch − a gift from Carla − said it was ten to nine.

There could only be one answer: that Carla had returned and, not wanting to wake me, had left me a note. Her towel was dry, all her clothes were in order and I had found no paper, no note, no sign, not even any money, let alone a message saying she had left me, that she couldn't bear me having another woman and confessing it to her.

At a quarter to ten I decided to go and look for her without further delay. Outside the *Terral*[12] was blowing and everywhere was dark, except the hotel lobby and the topmost windows of the Cohíba. I ordered a taxi. I was annoyed instantly at having to cough up for this expense. The trees in

Miramar[13] all leaned backwards in the darkness. Through the windshield, the occasional streetlight could be made out, casting an unearthly light against the austere, silent mansion behind it. I could barely see the palm trees on Calle 10.

The driver charged me four-fifty; the doorman ten bucks to get in. The sound of salsa thundered in my ears as I crossed the wide forecourt, and a shudder ran through me at the door. I was afraid, not only of not finding her, but of being in the dark generally: not being able to talk to her, or worse seeing her dancing there, carefree, and in that way defying my betrayal among these gold chain wearing men and dolled-up, dark-skinned women, with their blonde Beyonce fringes, among these young people and well-built male prostitutes with their baseball caps turned backwards, or among the ruthless magnates in sunglasses, prowling alone away from the dance floor, dressed in their denim and gabardine, as the musicians blow on their brass so hard the sound almost explodes, and the dancers, drenched in sweat, whirl so quickly and twist so violently, just to mark their steps.

But in the distance I saw her, between two spotlights at the back of the hall, close to the dance floor. And she saw me, and approached, smiling, pushing bodies out of her way. I felt a strange relief, as well as a sense of dejection, a vague rage against the suffocation of the place, which then began to subside as she drew towards me, her blonde hair swaying back and forth, sprinkling droplets of sweat, and dressed in a silk one-piece I'd never seen before – Prussian blue, sometimes shimmering, sometimes not – as her body undulated upwards from those strong legs and wide Moroccan-leather sandals. I composed myself, but felt my face tense even when the fear subsided. I wanted to shake her by the shoulders, and scream at her, but she placed her finger on my lips gently, then kissed me – more a caressing of the lips than a kiss – then slipped an arm round my waist, just as she might have done before, and, without apologising, she simply smiled and shouted, under the merciless clatter of the pailas,[14] that this encounter, like everything else, had all been planned; it had been part of the surprise she had wanted to give me at the end of the day; a surprise that was waiting for me, there at the edge of the dancefloor, at a table at the back, under the arc of lights; a surprise, or rather a wake-up call, that grew as we approached the ever-brightening light and I began to make out, through the dancers, in the gaps left between one body and the next, a flash of gold inlaid with ivory, and standing there: Tany, in a violet silk blouse I didn't recognise, looking a little scared at Carla, and me not yet understanding, until that very moment when I remembered their trip to the bathroom the night before, to touch up their make-up, returning so happy (so very happy). I tried to push Carla out of my way so I could get to the table first, but Carla got there first – she had always been ahead of me, it turned out – and kissed Tany shamelessly on the lips, embracing her. Tany allowed herself to be pulled in close as if, I don't know, as if she'd always been hers, since the day they'd met. Then I stopped, at the edge of the seats, sweaty and tired, beginning to comprehend the huge, unbridgeable chasm that had appeared between me and these two women, just about grasping, so late in the day, and with such awkwardness, that Tany was leaving me and that a true 'Ali Khan day' was about to begin for her.

Notes

1. Robaina, farming territory in Pinar del Río.

2. Zanja and Manrique, two large streets in the Chinatown area of Havana.

3. The Hotel Habana Riviera, also known as the Gran Caribe Habana Riviera, Hotel Riviera Havana or Havana Rivera, is located on the Malecón waterfront boulevard in the Vedado district of Havana, Cuba.

4. Eastern Cuban term meaning brother, buddy.

5. *Singer of Guaracha, Mexican music.*

6. Torre de Marfil, a Chinese restaurant.

7. Italian: *mare aperto - offshore*

8. An old bus, called "camel" because of its shape.

9. Sección de Intereses, as the US office was called, after the closure of the Embassy. The US Embassy was opened again in July 2015.

10. A well-known restaurant, named after Hemingway's Havana-set novel.

11. Panataxi - state run taxi service.

12. Terral - a land breeze.

13. Miramar - a residential district in the municipality of Playa, Havana, literally means 'sea view'.

14. Paila – a type of drum.

Diary of a Serial Killer in the Jurassic

Jorge Enrique Lage

AT THE CORNER OF Linea and Paseo, I met a brontosaurus.

It was dead.

(Genus: *Apatosaurus,* Order: *Saurischia ("Lizard-Hipped" Pelvic Structure),* Suborder: *Sauropod*).

It looked not dissimilar to a mountain of green dung.

Some kids were playing on top of the dung and from time to time they themselves looked green.

I asked whether one of them had killed it.

'We found it dead.'

'We're not assassins.'

'We haven't learnt how to kill things, yet.'

'September 16th. Today is the birthday of...'

The kid who said this was reading a hardback notebook with *South Park*'s Kenny McCormick on the cover. He looked a bit like Kenny himself but without the hood; his hair in a terrible mess, all covered in blood and slimy mud.

'Is that yours?' I asked him.

'Yes. I just found it in the brontosaurus' stomach.'

To think how far we've come and how far we're prepared to go to tell this tall tale.

You'll be famous when you grow up, I thought. *Or else, you'll be great, as a writer.*

'Let's make a deal.'

'One dollar,' the kid proposed.

I told him I could do better than that: a mint sweet. They too are green.

Kenny agreed. We shook on it and I left. Full stop.

Here is where all this begins.

I opened the notebook.

It was a diary.

September 16th

Today is the birthday of someone I thought I knew but didn't, someone who once advised me: 'Use everything you have.' I never knew what he meant by it, but I suspect it has some bearing on the chain of events I'm about to set in motion: a sequence of ideas destined to end up in the headlines and to make its way into legend. What I'm about to do is for myself and for the women but also, to a certain extent, for him. Happy birthday, you old bastard.

Does he imagine this is all I've got, the only thing I have!

Yes, I'm going to start with J. I just decided this. Not because she is a whore: they all are. I'll start with J because, that's the most perverse and '*heavy*'[1] way to start – the only real beginning. And he, wherever he is, knows what I'm talking about. He is a writer.

So I set out to find that two-storey house, with its fence and garden.

Continent Nuevo Vedado.[2]

Weeds covering the entire place.

Small rodent-like shapes, slipping through the undergrowth.

The door to J's house stood wide open, so I let myself in. I turned on the TV in the middle of a music video by Evanescence. I turned the volume up and went upstairs, and there she was, lying on the red sheets. Very naked, very pale: a little gothic doll, Amy Lee style. She was the type of woman you could imagine with a pneumatic drill in her hands, shattering the floor beneath your feet, while maintaining perfect make-up.

She looked at me, and didn't seem surprised.

Breathe into me and make me real.

Bring me to life.

'And who might you be?' she fluttered her eyelashes.

'Someone who always arrives too late.'

The blood had already dried on the sheets and her skin. I know because I got close enough to touch it. She let me touch it.

Now that I know what I'm without

you can't just leave me.

'You look exactly like someone I once loved to death,' she said. Then she asked: 'Where are you from?' I said I didn't know which 'where' she was referring to. (Time, planet, continent, fiction, truth, nightmare).

She clarified, her voice growing ever so soft: 'From which continent?'

Maybe she was just saying this to keep things simple.

'I'm not sure you and I use the same maps,' I said, and sat down beside her, thinking: *I should show her the diary so she can see there are clearly others like her, thankfully, she may have been the first but won't be the last.*

And I guess it's ciao for now, gorgeous. Don't know when. Don't know where.

But instead of saying goodbye, I just stood there silent, not with it, looking at her, then at the walls with their malevolent print (probably Japanese), then through the window at the small, rodent-like shapes on the branches of a tree.

'Primitive mammal,' she said.

'Primitive mammal,' I repeated.

October 1st

When I left K's house (if you can call a bundle of logs nailed up in the branches of a tree a 'house'), I found myself walking through streets that still brought me the fondest memories. I went to the Mónaco cinema, now a triple-X house, and watched a semi-humorous hardcore flick, starring Sheila Roche. No comment. But, you know, once in a while, a dose of something far removed from 'proper' cinema, something you'd never see in those arthouse movies, is healthy.

(Suite Habana notwithstanding).

This city's hellish climate probably resembles what the Earth must have been like many aeons ago – let's say 145 million years ago. The warmth and humidity drives you mad – as warm and humid as the women's bodies: their prehistoric bodies, that is to say their bodies in this prehistoric post-history. Mad.

From up there you could see all the roof terraces of a neighbourhood called La Vibora.

You could see the big hotels: hotels with casinos, hotels with helicopter landing pads on their roofs.

And as well as helicopters, you could see pterodactyls flying around.

(Order: Pterosauria – 11-to-12 metre wingspans: the largest flying creatures you can imagine).

Even if you weren't a person of faith, you could contemplate the lights of the tower of the Plaza de la Revolución with a sense of awe.

'I think I'm going to get off here,' said K. 'None of this makes sense anymore.'

I had been sitting (almost the whole time) beside a great chest made (like most other things) of wood, sifting through old postcards: Buenos Aires, Paris, Hong Kong. Chess moves, wedding proposals, confessions of every type and in every language. Seattle, Hiroshima, Istanbul – as many different handwriting styles as there are different cities around the world.

But none of these cities exist. Not yet.

'Just believe me when I tell you: you really do look a lot like him,' was the only comment K made after a long time spent engrossed in the uncivilised details of the diary. 'Physically, I mean.'

Now she was standing between the branches that acted as her doorway, telling herself that she was going to go down.

She turned her back to me and her see-through robe allowed me to inspect her back – quite free of blood – and allowed me to imagine her body without the stab wounds I'd just seen on her abdomen and breasts.

Just like that: the beautiful stab wounds.

And those despicable breasts.

'Let me go down first,' I suggested.

'You should try being alone for a while up here,' she replied.

I didn't want to try that. Just in case.

So she waited. She might have even gone down after me.

Maybe she was right; maybe nothing did make sense anymore.

OK then: so, if that's the case, all of the above doesn't make any sense either. The only thing you can be sure of is all meaning is lost in this image of a wooden shack built by a girl on top of a tree, in defiance of the whole world, almost at the beginning of time.

October 13th

Today I wandered under bridges and through the mouths of tunnels. I amused myself in these spaces, once created for the

Almendares to flow through, and decided to leave L for the morning. There are places like these – places you don't want to leave, where the city promises you something, and ends up not giving you, of course, but the promise is enough in itself. I have a map of these places.

Generally speaking, it's always important to have a map. Or more than one.

Tomorrow, I will look for L on the other side of the river, Fifth Avenue, and further inland. Hopefully no one will misinterpret what I am going to do; I wouldn't want to create a diplomatic incident. Somehow I know misinterpretation and erroneous readings will always follow me. I suspect one day these fragments will be found by someone who can't read at all.

L is a foreigner.

So am I, as it happens, but she is in the true sense of the word.

To be more specific, she lives in an embassy, in Miramar.

That is to say, when she was alive she did...

It's the embassy of a country which will come into being some 4 million years from now. Namely the United States of America.

'We have a friend in common,' I told her through the intercom on the street and, once inside, she told me:

'When I saw you from a distance, I thought you were him. I thought he was coming back to the scene of the crime, as the saying goes.'

Then I asked myself: *What the hell* was *I doing at the 'scene of the crime'*.

I guess because the place looked so familiar, insanely familiar, just like the others.

'You look...You *are* just like him, but you're not like him, right?'

'I don't know,' I replied. 'I met him but I didn't meet him, if you know what I mean. What was he like?'

'A bad guy. A 25-year-old teenager. One of those solitary types you love precisely because they're dangerous and you know they're incapable of loving you back.'

I didn't tell her how much I wished I fit that description.

I took the diary from her hands and kissed her. Her lips were cold. She pulled me towards a glass table, which crashed over as we clumsily undressed, spilling papers, pens and other office junk onto the floor. Her thighs were so cold and damp, her whole body below zero. Of course, I couldn't. I must have stuck my tongue into all her openings, especially those exposed by the knife's blade, but in the end I couldn't. She asked me to stop playing with her, she was fed up with games.

So was I.

And many other things besides.

L lifted up the glass table, and beneath it I saw a map of the Earth, and the Earth had two supercontinents – south and north – divided by a strip of sea whose western side was in the area of the Mediterranean.

L straightened her clothes and went back to reading. I felt something pressing against my foot and all of a sudden I found myself down on the ground, stroking a stego-baby.

A baby stegosaurus.

(Subgroup: thyreophora; commonplace armoured exterior with plates and spikes; fossil record: sparse)

'My pet!' L shouted down to me. 'I call her Daína Chaviano.'[3]

October 29th

It's strange to think I am writing this in a kid's notebook with a *South Park* character on the cover. A present from M, who told me: 'Writing is a therapy.' This morning, as I slid the blade out of one of her organs, I whispered in her ear: 'It is the worst of therapies.' She looked at me saying nothing (well, I had my other hand over her mouth) and died – just like that, eyes wide opened – a few seconds later.

I left all four of them with their eyes open. I'm sure of that.

Now their dying stares follow me everywhere, from McDonald's to the metro stations, backlit by neon light. As if the city were somehow aware – through them and like them – that something isn't quite working in my brain. I know it is the result of taking a certain irony to its limits, and beyond: to a new plane, a new paradigm. But this city's signature response is always rejection.

I almost walked the entire length of the Malecón.[4] In the distance, out at sea, a plesiosaurious lifted its head.

(Some species have a long neck and small head; others a short neck and big head).

I reached the correct building. The lift refused to work but, as it happened, I didn't have to climb all the way up to M's flat.

I found her sitting on the stairs.

Stairs that lead all the way up to the fake sky above Centro Habana.[5]

Climbing in the darkness. A torchlight. I covered my face with Kenny so the light wouldn't blind me.

'I know that notebook,' she said.

I asked her to turn off the light and turned to the first page, started reading.

She wouldn't have any of it. I tried to summarise key passages.

'So, I'm the fourth... and the last?'

'Sorry, I can't answer that one.'

I took my place beside her on the steps. We couldn't see

each other's faces but I knew her scent: she smelled like *Barbie* dreaming of being an actress.

'Dreams that have come true,' she informed me. Her name was going to be written in the annals of Cuban cinema – cinema that would bring us all out of this lethargy.

'I've just finished a film with Terence Piard.'

'He's dead,' I noted.

'So am I. It doesn't matter. It's the best film this country has ever produced!'

Her scent was that of a red-haired fashion model. Her hair recently washed. The blood diluted.

'What does a woman think about,' I ask, 'when she believes nothing and no one can hurt her?' I have no idea where this question came from. M didn't answer. The light from her torch blinded me. I closed my eyes and somehow, from her body to mine, all her trembling transferred to me... I could feel it.

'What does a serial killer think about,' she replied, 'when he believes he has left everything behind?'

I didn't respond either. A long time slipped by in those few seconds and then it was dark again, followed by the sound of her footsteps going upstairs, followed by silence.

I went out into the street.

A light rain fell on the Malecón.

For the fourth time in a row I had the feeling that everything had been too short, too late, too... nothing.

And I told myself: *too short, too late, too nothing.*

November 7th

Almost the 8th, actually, as it's nearly midnight. My hands are empty and I'm not tired anymore. A few hours ago I threw the knife as far out into the sea as I could. That is to say: several miles out. By now it must have reached the bottom, where no nice fish can be found, in the company of sunken galleons, balsa rafts, and nuclear submarines.

By the way, it was a Japanese knife. I'm not sure what that implies.

It's clear I'm not going to stop now. I thought about a new series, with no stab wounds. A different style, a different diary. There comes a time when you realise you have more things you can use, more than you thought, and you want to use them. Without delay! I think I'd only reach the end if something impossible happened to me, like dying of cold in Havana. Like being eaten by a dinosaur.

A reoccurring motif, I thought, the next time I saw that group of kids.

The structures seem to follow you even if you want to dismiss them as just ruins.

This time they were playing among the ruins of the Morro[6] and, from time to time, they themselves seemed like miniature ruins.

I didn't see Kenny McCormick with them. I figured he would be grown-up by then and would be living like a god.

A god with an orange hood, signing autographs in English.

It's true what they say: *Every generation has a legend.*

I started thinking about everything that distinguished me from those kids: *I am 25. I have memories. I have my desperation and my 'non-writing'.*

Enough is enough, I thought, and walked out in the low tide, as far as the reefs would let me, and threw the diary out into the sea.

A plesiosaur with a long neck and small head followed it with its eyes, caught it mid-air in its mouth and swallowed it.

Full stop.

Here is where this ends.
Anything else to say?

By the way, the other thing they say about this place is not true: the city I'm talking about, the location of those crime scenes, it's not an artificial paradise for reptiles.

For example: you won't find any T-rexes.

Nor any velociraptors.

Nothing like that.

We are not in the Cretaceous.

Notes

1. In English in the original.
2. The Nuevo Vedado neighbourhood in Havana, an upmarket residential area, settled in the 1930's and part of the Plaza de la Revolución municipality.
3. Daína Chaviano is a Cuban writer, born in 1957. She is considered one of the three most important female fantasy and science fiction writers in the Spanish language, along with Angélica Gorodischer (Argentina) and Elia Barceló (Spain).
4. The Malecón (officially Avenida de Maceo) is a broad esplanade, roadway and sea wall which stretches for 8km (5 miles) along the coast in Havana.
5. Centro Habana is one of the fifteen municipalities or boroughs in the city of Havana.
6. Morro Castle, Spanish: Castillo de los Tres Reyes Magos del Morro, named after the three biblical Magi, is a fortress guarding the entrance to Havana bay in Havana.

The List

Ahmel Echevarría Peré

*'The dead and my friends (you among them) appear to me
in dreams. This is the way things are at my age: to meet
with people you love it is necessary to sleep.'*
– Artificial Respiration, Ricardo Piglia

1.

'TAKE ME OFF "THE LIST"!' Toni said.

We had met in a bookshop midweek. He was suggesting I remove his name from the list we'd compiled. It was a Wednesday. It was 7pm in the evening. In a working week, Wednesday is slap bang in the middle, sort of stuck between a rock and a hard place.

'I'm leaving the country, maybe in the next month or two, not sure, or in the next year. Or maybe never.'

I laughed, then realised he wasn't laughing. Toni didn't laugh.

'Take me off, just in case.'

He put his hand on my shoulder.

We parted with a hug. Firm, but also sentimental.

'Don't forget Ahmel: cross me off! But leave an X!'

I didn't feel like watching him retrace his steps down San Rafael Boulevard, picking his way through the pedestrians, the left-out rubbish, and the dog shit, at 7.30 on a Wednesday night, all the way till he reached the 222 or 298 bus stop. So I

87

left myself. Gathering momentum, I set off: San Rafael towards Campanario. People, rubbish, the smell of reheated oil frying chickens and croquettes somewhere, potholes, more rubbish, dog shit. I was walking in the opposite direction to Toni.

I left reflecting that Wednesday is indeed a day stuck between a rock and a hard place: the bookshop air conditioner having been the only pleasant thing from morning to night.

This guy had a wife and a son, by the way: a wife who looked like him – like Toni, I mean – but the baby was cute. European and cute.

2.

Alexis had managed to circle a quarter of the globe already. As far as I knew. Centro Habana to Madrid, to Canasí,[1] to London, to Pinar del Río,[2] to the Vatican, to Paris, to New York, to Matanzas.[3]

It was always Centro Habana he flew from (Havana–World, World–Havana).

One thing Alexis will pack up in his luggage is a date. The sixteenth of June, 1998. Al will never forget that night.

> *I, being born at the sharp end of the sword,*
> *being myself, without Damocles, without history,*
> *I renounce my time to kill,*
> *I renounce my peace and I stay:*
> *native of a besieged city*
> *not by virtue*
> *of surviving adrift on the tide.*
> *I testify that I feel disadvantaged...*

he wrote one night in his house, at the corner of Belascoain, Centro Habana.

Al had got an opportunity to take another trip to New York, the Big Apple. That huge, sprawling, cosmopolitan apple. The plunge couldn't be delayed any further; José Martí Airport on a rainy day. But this time it was persistent rain; 'persistent enough to fit in a bolero'.[4] Persistent (adjective, feminine): stubborn, tenacious, a synonym for obstinate and, in a figurative sense: relentless. Thus was the downpour: violent and stubborn; more than violent, endless.

Our friend Lena said that Alexis' departure would be just another adventure. I said no, she was wrong. We discussed it at length, with growing intensity. Al was an old friend.

'Shall we bet on it?' I asked her in the end.

So far, I'm winning.

3.

Lena dreamed of being a producer. Film production was her destiny, her '*derrotero*' –meaning 'course', the route that guides a ship, according to the *Petit Larousse*. Coming and going – that's what Lena wanted, to travel yet return..., interminably, in an eternal cycle. Forever.

Lena couldn't deviate from her course. In her case, the intersection between the streets L and 17 – the corner where she lived – would serve as launch pad for the jump (Havana-World, World-Havana), and El Vedado would act as base camp for all explorations. All uniform and circular trajectories, God willing.

El Vedado: just a phase in the cycle. Was that possible?

I wouldn't want to bet on it.

4.

The List

1. Ernesto (automated systems engineer, Stockholm, two children)
2. Leonardo (automated systems engineer, Stockholm, two children)
3. Orlando (former microbiologist, now writer)
4. Alexis (literature teacher, New York)
5. Lena (industrial engineer, film producer)
6. Mylai (graduate in law, Mexico Districto Federal, teaches in a prison)
7. Toni (mechanical engineer; maybe one day he'll move to Barcelona?)
8. Towie (visual artist and aikido teacher)
9. Andrés (economics graduate, presently processing departure papers, has bribed half of Havana; future destination: Dresden)
10. Ahmel (mechanical engineer; maybe one day he'll move to Barcelona?)
11. Yani (degree in law)
12. Pavel (industrial designer, London)
13. Karem (doctor)
14. Pedro Bandera (drummer, Sao Paulo)
15. Vania (philologist)
16. Edith (degree in art history)

Making an inventory of friends is not a healthy exercise. It's easier to simply bring them all together at midnight. But compiling the list is less cruel and actually fun. I daydream and, in that dream, I assemble them all in one place, or those that fit the dream at least, and it doesn't tire me. I daydream, until the point where I'm used to their company again, and I know I won't miss them when they go back to Stockholm, Sao Paulo, London or New York.

5.

Yani doesn't like the idea of leaving her mother alone.

Yani and her mother need to finish work on the house. Their house. They are building it without God's help.

6.

For 'The List' I would need different types of ink. Three colours were required. Blue, red and green would be convenient.

'Blue, red and green?' my mother asked.

'Yes, that's the combination.'

She looked at me, puzzled. We were standing on the balcony of the apartment.

'What are you talking about?' she asked. 'Hang on, your grandmother's calling.'

In the list, I would use blue for those who no longer walked the streets of *my* Havana. The choice of blue was not accidental. The colour blue, as well as maybe misty-white, represented what is far away. Those who were currently waiting for their passports and papers to be processed would be written in green letters. Red ink, meanwhile, stood for the potential emigrants.

'Mum! Do they even sell red pens anymore?'

'I don't know!'

'Mum, would you emigrate?'

She didn't want to answer, just looked away.

Writing a letter is not a healthy exercise either. Those no longer living in *my* Havana are like ghosts to me. They appear without being summoned. They are tormented souls. 'The List' would be a kind of Mass, for them, bringing them, or me, some peace. Al would be blue; Toni green, Lena red. Pavel, Pedro Bandera, Mylai, Ernesto and Leonardo would also be blue; Andrés green; Yani red... I'd need to guess the others, but I know Towie's would be red.

What colour would I use to write my own name?

Ahmel:.... red.

Too many ghosts flying around.

Ernesto came from Sweden and brought me a gift.

'It's symbolic,' he said.

Now I'm someone who owns a walkman. I don't know how else to put it. A man with a music player, walking through the city. Havana appears like a video clip now, but it is more than that. I listen to Tracy Chapman. I run. I board the metrobus, in a crowd of others struggling to squeeze on. A man and a woman fight for their place in the queue, then their place along the aisle, and finally about his ass touching hers, even though he's doing his best to give her ass room.

On the sidewalk, a woman is wiping sweat from her brow. She looks at me through the glass then sidesteps into the shade of a kiosk serving drinks. Too much heat; too much humidity. She looks like she's about to faint. From one of the kiosk's few occupied tables, someone stares at her, while having a beer to cool themselves down. But she has to keep going. I'm transported along on wheels while the woman walks; we reach the traffic light slowly together, sweating. A motorcade is crossing the street, and the police have halted traffic. Yellow school buses, yellow buses with black stripes, yellow buses full of foreign students. *Don't you know / they're talkin' about a revolution / it sounds like a whisper* –Tracy sings. And I just start to get hot: too much heat and music, piercing the ears and the skin. In the *guagua*[5] arms flap up and down like in an endless pantomime. Flags are waved, many paper flags, rippling in the currents of the air. From the foreign students' bus, a few cameras and phones film the crowded metrobus alongside them. They capture the poverty of the vehicle, and its passengers. Then the foreign students overtake us, looking to me as if utterly struck dumb. *It sounds like a whisper* – I hear on my walkman. *It's true*, I think. They are so excited, they film, they wave, some even shout, but I can't hear them. So I guess they're just whispers.

I am walking in Centro Habana: the bedrock, the place where I last hugged Toni, this epicentre of the Earth for Al. Two men, dressed in blue – with a dog for company – are at the corner. I begin to sweat. They look at me. As I hum to myself, the policemen say something to me, but I can't hear them. They're checking papers, they look at me again, sweating themselves. The city has only one sound: that of my walkman. *Baby can I hold you tonight.* I think: *Hold her, hold Yani today*. I cross in front of the policemen and the dog. I glow with sweat as I walk. One of the policemen crosses his arms and the other walks up to me, with papers but without the dog. *Baby can I hold you tonight* – I thought I heard. The other bends down, strokes the dog's back, looks at me and laughs. Hold her? I'd like to *kiss* my girlfriend today. *Yani, can I hold you today?* The policeman tells me to stop, but then simply asks the time. Laughing at me, there on the pavement, he adjusts his weapon, then his beret, then strolls back to where his partner is waiting.

The policemen move their lips. Again I hear nothing. The music fades out. I keep going. *You're so lucky!* I think. I have an impulse to stop and turn around. Ahead of me, I can see the dog sniffing at the wall of a house, he lifts his leg and pisses.

Before I know it, they are behind me, far, far behind, in the distance.

I imagine my body as a red spot in the middle of the masses. I walk among a tide of other dots, of different colours. We are out of sync – the tide and I. I imagine everything from above: not the city, just part of it, this stretch of Zanja Street, between Escobar and Campanario.

I feel as though I am walking but I'm not moving forward. Everything looks the same to me: the city is the same colour everywhere, dirty. It does not seem to belong to the tropics anymore. Where have the colours gone? Two shadows – a woman and a man – step in front of me. They're carrying rucksacks and bottled water, taking photos. What is it that I can't see?

I reach the intersection. I am finally there, at the corner of Zanja and Campanario. It's grey also. One last turn; a few metres and that's it. Part of my journey has ended. Yani has been waiting for me there, in her apartment. Afterwards, I will return to my flat.

7.

Havana, 16 June, 2000.

Al:

Ricardo Piglia[6] once described correspondence as a perverse genre that needs distance in order to thrive.[7] So I'm there, in one place, and *she*, the letter, is on its way to another. The letter is so much like a woman, a woman that might feature in a *bolero*. She comes and goes: 'deceitful', a *bolero* singer would say; gentle or cruel, between drunken harmonies and sobbing notes. I wait for it, or I don't. And then it comes, it staves in my hull, and I start to take on water. Correspondence always opens up a rupture. Friends writing to me reappear again after midnight, they sneak through the gaps. When I sleep, or when it's raining, they make their rounds. That's the point when I start to take on water, a lot of water. I risk running aground. In fact, I do run aground. It's just a piece of paper, another one to add to the pile: the trail of ink and crumpled sheets to satisfy the appetite of this creature of the *bolero*. 'Letters owed', was Piglia's phrase; a necessary Mass, I say. The analgesic in the small hours, in between the downpours, the Sunday afternoon downpours. Medication to kill this animal. Sadness takes advantage of the most ordinary moments and places.

I am taking on water. Cornered, I think. Both her – the letter – and I. She is slender and insubstantial, only stays a while, then she folds up and disappears.

PS: Correspondence is a perverse genre... it might have been me who first wrote that. I am sorry, I'm in no mood for this any more.

8.

11:59pm.
    I review 'The List'.
    I'll need to write a letter to Toni soon.

Notes

1. Arcos de Canasí is a small town in the east of the La Habana Province of Cuba.

2. Pinar del Río is a Cuban city, capital of Pinar del Río Province.

3. Matanzas is the capital of the Cuban province of Matanzas.

4. A Cuban expression; the word 'persistent' in Spanish fits into the 2/4 time signature of the bolero.

5. Guagua: the name people in Havana give to the local bus.

6. Ricardo Piglia (1941–2017): Argentine author, critic, and scholar best known for introducing hard-boiled fiction to the Argentine public.

7. Cited from *Artificial Respiration* (*Respiración artificia*), by Ricardo Piglia, 1980.

Of Princesses and Dragons

Irina J. Davidenko

ONCE UPON A TIME, there was a little girl who dreamed about a prince, a dragon, a winged stallion, a castle in the clouds, and long, long hair. Every night it was the same dream, every morning the same images running through her head: a towering castle, reaching beyond the highest clouds; a thousand sighs rising up from the moat where a dragon lay coiled – its skin only lukewarm, now, from having slumbered so long guarding the princess, with one eye open like a knife wound, but deep down, inside, still burning with the dragonfire that will never go out.

The princess casts her long braid from the turret like a scarf, which soars upwards on the thousand sighs, until it catches the attention of the brave prince, riding his winged stallion, summoning him to fly over the moat, dodge the dragon's many intakes of breath, and deliver the kiss that will set her free. There he is, already visible in the distance! He arrives at night, circumnavigating the stars, gliding down corridors of air. Like a breeze.

A prince on horseback, a dragon-slaying prince, rallying to defend this castle in the clouds! The night sky now lit up with bolts of fire from his sword, and from the beating of white wings – those thick, scaly, webbed wings. The princess cries out, but her voice is lost in the frenzied roar of the dragon bellowing its thousand sighs into detonations, exploding one by one. The princess falls into the void, calls out once more, cries and then laughs when a gloved hand appears from nowhere and grabs the long braid, Pegasus' soft back breaking her fall. The prince tightens her long hair in his manly glove and delivers the eternal kiss. The end. The dream always ends in the same place.

But, what happened next?

You have to eat the dragon to survive. You have to repair the castle, brick by brick, sand and cement, to put your own thousand sighs back together. The princess will need to cut her long braid and sell it to the wig makers. You'll need a few litres of oil to roast the dragon. Building supplies. A prince who's prepared to rent his winged horse out for weddings and birthday parties. Then buy a fridge to store the dragon portions, they'll start to stink otherwise. Your hands will become callused, your sighs will turn to bricks and mortar. After that: a guided tour of the castle in the clouds, free entrance for the kids on Sundays. The dragon meat is finished. What are we going to eat now? The children?

I took out the €100 and handed it to the cashier at the CADECA[1] – I always get the one talking on the phone about her boyfriend, filing her nails while simultaneously counting the notes. Impressive, being able to do everything at once like that, without losing count. A vision in lycra, glamour and indifference! I passed her the €100 that had been sweated for, and earned on the many Sundays when no kids showed up at the castle. I handed it over as if it was theirs. But in reality it was mine... and yours, my princess. And now, how am I going to explain this?

Look, darling, do you remember those friends I met during the trip – the man who promised me... yes, the head of the mission, that's the one. And his wife, of course.

Well, nothing. Remember I told you they were coming to Cuba, visiting, as tourists, the largest of the Antilles islands, darling? No, no, nothing to do with the job, although it always has something to do with it, doesn't it? So you say.

Well, they wrote to me and I offered to help them. To make sure they got a first class holiday. One hand washes the other, help and you'll be helped, people always appreciate being looked after. Isn't that what you told me, darling?

Well, I got skinned: I rang agencies, agents, guides, drivers; I bargained on prices, the works; everything you said I needed to learn how to do. I met them at the hotel. I organised things so they could pay me direct and didn't need to waste precious time going from agency to agency: I said I'd deal with everything. You would have been proud of your prince, darling.

I saddled my Pegasus – in reality a Moskovich,[2] or rather what was patched together from one, a *'Monster-vich'* – and set off to meet them.

Hotel Nacional de Cuba! I didn't say anything to you because I wanted to surprise you. I was sure that, in return for my services, my valuable support, that is to say my collaboration at the highest level, I would receive an invitation. Dinner at the tower. Not just any tower, my darling: the highest building in Havana,[3] the bird of Cuba, the tower with the thousand windows opening up the world to as many perspectives, with a thousand lights beaming from its sides. Our *Tower of Sighs.* There, I would have been your hero once more. Well, this would have happened eventually, my darling, but let me get there first.

Hotel Nacional de Cuba! Handshakes, slacks, sandals, summer dresses, relaxed vibes, the aroma of the sea, those wonderful gardens overlooking the bay, traditional music, and the palm trees slightly dishevelled from having enjoyed the wind and the son[4] too much. Me with my best shirt on, my best smile, ready with a comprehensive tour plan: Marina Hemingway, tobacco factory, salsa classes. Showering benevolence, *Noooooooo, you shouldn't have!* The lady is charmed, so is the gentleman..., darling, I mean, the head of the mission.

So they said they couldn't pay me in cuc,[5] because the hotel reception could only change €100 per client. Might I be able to change it for them? I knew there was a casa de cambio beside the pool, although the couple staffing it seemed too lazy to be of any use. Well, they didn't say that openly, but that's what I surmised.

'Of course, no problem, I'll handle this,' I reassured the tourists. 'That's what I'm here for. Let's check the exchange rate.' The man's mobile had a calculator – so handy, a real gem of a model. 1704 cuc rounded up to €1,320 they said, handing me the bills.

'No, I can't take that,' I insisted. 'It's more euros than I need. Now I owe you 6 cuc.'

'It doesn't matter,' they replied.

'Of course it matters,' I insisted, 'are you trying to tip me?'

I chuckled to myself. Who does anything out of friendship these days? I took out the small change I had in my pocket for petrol, and gave it to them to make things even. 'Please count the money *first*,' they said. And I went, 'It's okay, guys, no need for that.'

There was a tall black guy in a security uniform standing behind me, no doubt catching every word. He had such a face, darling, such eyes! And he was using one of those black walkie-talkies, the ones that always make your voice sound strange and start each sentence with a *sssshhh*. I wasn't unnerved by the man so much as his walkie-talkie, well, that and his beige uniform, and his sombre expression.

You get where I'm going with this. Who was I to be handling all this money for the tourists? I started to feel nervous. 'The money's fine,' I said to the couple quickly. 'Everything's cool. Enjoy your stay. Any problem, call me. This is my card.'

'On Saturday, we will expect you and your wife for dinner,' they said, inviting me to eat dragon, with you, honey.

'Call me,' I said. 'I know a great place.' *A Tower*, I wanted to whisper in the guy's ear.

'Of course. We'll call and confirm the time.' A handshake and a kiss from the lady.

I left like a rocket – as fast as my white 'Monster-vich' and the ever-widening potholes would allow. On Saturday, my princess will dine out: the date we put aside was now back on the agenda, after this new feat. Indeed it would be even more sumptuous! The prince had triumphed once again. He had defeated the dragon – the black man in uniform, and everything else. Once more, the hero would grab hold of the braid.

I pulled up at the first casa de cambio I could find. I couldn't risk trying the one by the hotel pool. That walkie-talkie had made me anxious.

So there I was, standing in front of a girl on the phone talking about her boyfriend, filing her nails, and not even looking at me, as I counted out the money to be changed. There, facing this fortress of indifference, the whole world seemed to collapse: my horse lost its wings. Darling, I was €100 short. A hundred euros! I'm sorry. I must have been nervous and not counted the money properly when they gave it to me. I'd glanced at this huge wad in my shaky hands, and thought it looked okay. Such a nice feeling, having these notes in my hands: crisp, soft, so new they were sharp enough to give you paper cuts. On top of that, the guy with the walkie-talkie, his uniform, I mean.

I thought of going back to talk to the man, the head of the mission, I swear I did. But I couldn't. I couldn't admit my defeat, my incompetence, neither to you nor them. As a vision, the magnificent dinner with roasted dragon was within sight. But I couldn't say anything. From the casa de cambio, I could see the Tower, but could I reach it anymore?

I drove home and grabbed the €100 we had been saving to fix the bathroom, or buy you new shoes, or was it a dress? Well, for something. I took it and handed it over to the girl who kept filing her nails and was now talking about her cousin's boyfriend. Still talking, nail file in hand, she counted the money: €1320 now – that's it. That was right, darling. It doesn't matter, I'll explain it to you.

I paid the agencies, the guides, the drivers; I paid for everything and I rang the hotel many times and left messages and... Saturday passed, Sunday passed. And I know that today, being Monday, their flight must have left already. Very friendly, sure they were. But we won't eat dragon any time soon, and the Tower will remain a dream. Plus, you won't have new shoes nor tiles for the bathroom. I still don't remember what that money was for. What's more, you'll no longer feel pride in this man you once dreamt of as a prince, who turned out to be just... me.

Notes

1. CADECA (casa de cambio) is the official government exchange house in Cuba where citizens can exchange foreign currencies into Cuban Convertible Pesos (CUC).

2. A pun on the word 'Moscovich' - the name of an old Soviet car.

3. This is a reference to the FOCSA Building which, at 121 metres high, is the tallest building in Cuba. Located in the Vedado neighbourhood of Havana, it was built in 1956.

4. Son, is probably the most well-known Cuban style of music and dance. The *son* constitutes one of the basic forms of Cuban music and is the basis of many Cuban genres and styles, among them the *salsa*. The most ancient *son* date back to the XVI century. The *son* was declared Cuban Cultural Heritage in 2012.

5. The Cuban Convertible Peso (CUC) is the primary official legal currency in Cuba.

You're Leaving Then

Cinthia R. Paredes

'SO. YOU'RE LEAVING THEN?'

Victor watches as she swallows her drink in one go, tilts her head back and lets it slide down of its own accord, then looks him in the eye.

'Yes.'

He had met her just two weeks ago, here on the Malecón, this promenade of a thousand peddlers. Some dumbass was trying to sell her an obviously stolen camera: 'I don't want it,' she was saying.

'Come on, lady, it's brand-new,' he persisted.

'You've just stolen it. I'm no fool,' she retorted.

'No, girl. It belongs to my cousin's wife.'

'I don't want it!'

'Then buy a present for your Dad, girl.' At this point Victor stepped in: 'Enough of this shit, *asere*.[1] Get the fuck out of here.' In an instant, the guy had disappeared and Victor realised he himself would have tried to sell her something just to be rewarded with the smile she was now giving him. At first he felt uncomfortable. She had thanked him, but continued to stare out into the distance and the faded edge where the sea ended. Not knowing what to do, he resorted to bribery.

'Like some peanuts?'

'I'm allergic.'

'A beer?'

'If you buy me a Bucanero,[2] I'll stay with you until morning.'

And there was light.

'You know, I dreamt about you last night.'

She shakes her head and smiles. What a silly boy! She had warned him not to fall in love with her; and she had warned herself as well. She could not fall in love, not even with the sweet little boy hiding behind this macho facade. When the time comes, there must be no doubt.

'Don't tell me what it was about, in case it comes true.'

The first time she asked him to take her home she thought everything would be fine. She didn't count on the lack of support from her immigrant family, fed up as they were, of readjusting themselves time and time again to the eight square metres they had to live in.

'You didn't bring this guy here to stay the night? Surely you didn't?'

'No, Mum. He just walked me home.'

'This guy is not a *yuma*.'[3]

'No, Uncle. He's not.'

'Then why in hell's name are you bringing a hungry-looking Cuban home, girl?'

A cousin chips in: 'Alicia, please. Learn from your sister: she brings the *yumas* here and takes the Cubans to the park.'

Alicia fell silent, she wanted to hide her head in shame, but the narrowness of the living room didn't even allow her to do that.

She shoved her way past them, retrieved a flask of rum from under her bed, took Victor by the arm, and left. What a dingy fucking dump: Centro Habana – where there isn't even enough room to feel shame.

'I really like the sound you make when you take a long sip,' Victor said as they swigged from the flask out in the street.

It was like a little snore, a *purring* that reminded him of the sound of a pulley, like the ones they used to lift furniture in old buildings during removals. It was like that, a gentle wheel embedded in the rafters of this old, flaking city.

'You'll miss it, that's for sure.'

Was he really so dumb? How could he keep sitting there with her, not knowing from one moment to the next whether she was about to disappear? How long could he go on fooling himself, when he knew deep down it would all be in vain? What did he expect? All his sins forgiven?

Two weeks. Two fucking weeks and he was so infatuated with this immigrant Bucanero-drinker that even his clothes felt like they were on fire.

He was so taken by her smile that, when he saw her that day in the Plaza Vieja, he *still* couldn't get annoyed with her. 'Alicia...,' he stuttered, 'How... who... how are you?"

To which she coolly replied: '*George, this is my sister's boyfriend.*'[4]

'Si, si, yes, yes,' he caught on quickly.

'Tell my sister I won't be sleeping at home today. Would you?' she kept the act going.

'*Si, si*. I mean, yes, yes,' he said, trying his best, as George grabbed her ass and audibly whispered:

'*I'm gonna fuck you all night long.*'[5]

Motherfucking love! Stopping him from getting annoyed when he should have! Dumb moronic love! Letting her slip back into his bed a couple of days later. What bullshit. What beautiful bullshit!

'What are you going to do, Victor, when I go?'

'I'll miss you.'

'Some day you'll stop missing me.'

'Only if you don't go, Alicia.'

How many times would they go over the same thing? There was no point. She was never going to stay and he was never going to stop asking her right up until the end. She didn't understand that.

'Do you remember the day...'

'Are you in love with him? With George?'

'...when we went to the Latino[6] and couldn't get in?'

'Or are you going with him because he can get you out of your eight square metres?'

'... so, with the bottle of rum and a ball of toilet paper, we staged our own match: Industriales versus Santiago?'[7]

'Do you really want to go?'

How well can a man know a woman, or a woman a man, in two weeks? In fourteen days? In three hundred and thirty-six hours?

Defying the so-called (but actually non-existent) rulebook, they had allowed themselves to merge, one with the other, without even leaving a crack through which to escape back to reality. A reality as naked as a piece of meat dripping over a butcher's table in a market. A reality that, having pounced on them, was now forcing them into this cramped, filthy corner marked *Way Out*.

'Victor, I'm leaving. Even if George was the most disgusting, meanest guy in the world...'

'You know tomorrow there is the opening of a new exhibition at the Cuba Pavillon.'

'...Even if they gave me a three-storey house, a 128 square metres...'

'...And Friday, Raul Paz is playing at Club 23.'

'...Even if I adore and love every inch of you...'

'Alicia...'

'...I am leaving. Nothing will make me change my mind.'

The blood curdled in his veins as she spoke these words. He couldn't win. Defeat had to be accepted, along with the kiss she let fall on his lips as he watched her depart, so straight, so determined that he finally understood.

'So. You are leaving, then.'

Notes

1. Asere comes from the sacred Efik language greeting of the Afro-Cuban Abaku religion, meaning literally, 'I salute you.' Today, it is a common greeting among young Cubans. Meaning friend, buddy, mate.

2. A Cuban brand.

3. Yuma, a Cuban term meaning American and by extension, foreigner. It comes from the 1957 film starring Glenn Ford and Van Heflin, "3:10 to Yuma". Yuma is a city in Arizona, near the border with Mexico.

4. In English in the original.

5. In English in the original.

6. The Latino Baseball Stadium: The Estadio Latinoamericano ('Latin American Stadium') opened on October 26, 1946, and was renovated and expanded in 1971, primarily used for baseball, but has also occasionally been used for political rallies.

7. *Industriales* is a baseball team in the Cuban National Series. Santiago de Cuba is also a baseball team in the Cuban National Series.

About the Authors

Daniel Chavarria was born in Montevideo, Uruguay, in 1933. He lived in Cuba for over forty years and considered himself a Cuban. Although prolific and diverse in his output, he was perhaps best known for his detective and thriller novels, set against the backdrop of various political events. His novels included: *Joy* (1978, Cuba); *Una Pica en Flandes* (2006, Cuba); *Viudas de Sangre* (2004, Cuba); *El Ojo de Cibeles* (Letras Cubanas, 2012, Cuba), *La Sexta Isla* (new edition, Capitan San Luis, 2012, Cuba). His many literary prizes included: the Literature Cuban Nacional Prize and its equivalent in Uruguay, the Bartolomé Hidalgo Prize, in 2010, as well as the Casa de las Américas Prize and the Hammet (United States) for the best detective novel of 2014 - *Allá ellos* (1991, Cuba). In 2005, he won the Edgar Allan Poe Award (presented by the Mystery Writers of America) for the novel *Adiós muchachos* (1994, Cuba). He also won the Camilo José Cela (Spain) in 2003, and the Casa de las Américas (2000) and the Alejo Carpentier Prize (2004). On 6 April 2018, just as this book was being sent to print, Chavarria passed away.

Irina J. Davidenko was born in Russia in 1978, to a Cuban father and Russian mother. She moved to Havana in 1982 where she completed her education. Davidenko studied for a degree in Economics but after graduating in 2003 began her career as a theatre actress. She has been awarded several prizes for her acting as well as for her audiovisual work. She is the author of a number of plays as well as short stories. Her play *Manada* was performed by the company Rita Montaner (directed by Fernando Quiñones), and she is part of the group Teatro D'dos directed by Julio César Ramírez. She regularly publishes articles in theatre magazines, including *Tablas* and *Conjunto*. Together with other young writers she founded a creative writing group in Havana, and is currently writing a script for a workshop given by The Royal Court of London.

Laidi Fernández de Juan was born in Havana, Cuba, in 1961. A writer and doctor, she has worked many years in Cuban medical missions, especially in Africa. She began her literary career in 1994 with a collection of short stories, *Dolly y otros cuentos africanos* (Letras Cubanas, 1994, Cuba). She writes a regular column, called *Cosas del caos* in the literary magazine *Cuba Contemporánea*. She also writes regularly for the online magazine *La Jiribilla* and runs a meeting space at the Cultural Centre Dulce Maria Loynaz called 'Wednesdays of Smiles'. She has published ten books, among them: *Oh Vida* (Editorial Unión, 1998, Cuba), which was awarded the Premio Nacional de Cuentos 'Luis Felipe Rodríguez'; *La hija de Darío* (Letras Cubanas, 2005, Cuba); *Bésame mucho* (2007, Ediciones Banda Oriental, Montevideo, Uruguay); *Universo y la lista* (2013, Ediciones Matanzas, Cuba); *Jugada en G* (Unión, 2013, Cuba); and *Será siempre* (2014, Ediciones Holguin, Cuba), her first collection of 'mini short stories'.

Jorge Enrique Lage was born in Havana, Cuba, in 1979. He has a degree in biochemistry and is a writer and journalist. He studied at the Jorge Onelio Cardoso where he also now works, coordinating their publishing activity. He regularly contributes to various Cuban literary magazines, as well as foreign media outlets. He has published several short story collections: *Yo fui un adolescente ladrón de tumbas* (Ediciones Extramuros, La Habana, 2004), *Fragmentos encontrados en La Rampa* (Editora Abril, La Habana, 2004), *Los ojos de fuego verde*

(Editora Abril, La Habana, 2005), *El color de la sangre diluida* (Editorial Letras Cubanas, La Habana, 2008), and *Vultureffect* (Ediciones Unión, La Habana, 2011). He has also published the novels *Carbono 14. Una novela de culto* (Ediciones Altazor, Lima, 2010; Editorial Letras Cubanas, La Habana, 2012), *La autopista: the movie* (Editorial Caja China, La Habana 2014) and *Archivo* (Editorial Hypermedia, Madrid, 2015).

Eduardo Heras León was born in Havana, Cuba, in 1940. He is a highly renowned Cuban writer, as well as a journalist and critic of literature and ballet. He holds a degree in journalism and philology and is the founder and director of the prestigious Jorge Onelio Cardoso Centre. He is a writer belonging to the Revolution generation, involved in and committed to the revolutionary process since 1959. His many books include: *La guerra tuvo seis nombres* (Unión, 1968, Cuba); *Los pasos en la hierba* (Casa de Las Américas,1970, Cuba); *Acero* (Arte y Literatura,1977, Cuba), *Dolce vita* (Unión, 2012, Cuba). He was awarded the National Literature Prize (Cuba) in 2014. Other prizes include: UNEAC 1983, and Casa de Las Américas Prize in 1970 for *Los pasos en la hierba*.

Eduardo del Llano was born in Moscow, Russia, in 1962. A well-known writer, script writer, film director and actor, del Llano has studied Art History at the University of Havana. His novels include: *Los doce apóstatas* (Editorial Letras Cubanas, 1994, Cuba); *Obstáculo* (Editorial Letras Cubanas, 1997, Cuba); and *Tres* (colección La Novela, Editorial Letras Cubanas, 2002, Cuba) - later published in Austria, Spain and Columbia. Among other prizes, he was awarded the Italo Calvino Prize 1996. As a film director he is well known for his series of short films called *Cuentos of Nicanor*, which are often based on his own short stories. Both his writing and his films are renowned for their subtle sense of humour, and a literary register that swings effortlessly between the highly cultivated to the highly colloquial. He is the founder and director of the creative writing group, NOS-Y-OTROs.

Ahmel Echevarría Peré was born in Havana, Cuba, in 1974. One of Cuba's most acclaimed younger writers, he was a student at the Jorge Onelio Cardoso Centre for Literary Formation, where he now works as the editor of its website. He is also editor of the website *Vercuba*, and writes a column in the literary magazine *Cuba Contemporánea*. His books include: *Inventario* (Unión, 2007, Cuba), the short novel *Esquirlas* (Letras Cubanas, 2006, Cuba); *Búfalos camino al matadero* (Oriente, 2013, Cuba); and *La noria* (Unión, 2013, Cuba). He was awarded the David Unión prize in 2004 for his book *Inventario* and The Franz Kafka Novelas de Gaveta Prize in the Czech Republic 2011 for his book *Dias de entrenamiento*, also awarded the Italo Calvino Prize 2012. His book *La Noria* was awarded the Critic Prize 2013.

Cinthia R. Paredes was born in Havana, Cuba, in 1982. She is a writer and actress, and holds a degree in education and English Language. Paredes has been part of the Rita Montaner Company for eight years, and is the director of the documentary *Desde un Sotano*. She began her creative career as writer of fiction over ten years ago, but left for a period to concentrate on theatre work. Her work *ES-3S* has been performed under the direction of Fernando Quiñones, and *Bruk, the Last Troll*, has been performed by the company JazzVila, directed by Vila. She is currently writing a script for a workshop given by The Royal Court of London.

Francisco López Sacha was born in Manzanillo, Cuba, in 1950. He is a writer, essayist and teacher. He is editor of the literary magazine *Letras Cubanas* and a professor at the prestigious School of Cinema of San Antonio de Los Baños. He has been writing fiction since 1977 and in 1986 he published his first novel, *El cumpleaños del fuego* and a year later his first short story collection: *La división de las aguas* (Letras Cubanas, 1987, Cuba); the latter was awarded the Caimán Barbudo Prize. In 1988 he published a second collection of short stories, *Análisis de la ternura* (Ediciones Unión, 1988, Cuba). He has also published numerous collections of essays, including *La nueva cuentística cubana* (1994) and *Pastel flameante* (2006), and edited two anthologies of Cuban short stories: *Fábula de ángeles: antología de nuevos narradores cubanos* (1994), and *La isla contada: el cuento cubano contemporáneo* (1996), the latter having since been translated into Portuguese and Italian. He has been president of the UNEAC (Writers and Artists Union).

Eduardo Angel Santiesteban was born in Havana, Cuba, in 1997. He is currently studying at the University Obrero Campesina. At the age of just 16, he was invited to take part in the prestigious fiction course run by the Jorge Onelio Cardoso Centre of Literary Formation. He was also awarded the "creation bursary" *El caballo de coral*, for his 'novel in progress' which he is currently developing. He is part of a generation of very young writers known as the "children of the Special Period" (the decade 1990–2000 when the economic crisis, due especially to the fall of the Soviet Union, hit Cuba hard) – young authors who have just begun to appear on the literary scene and depict a very different Cuba from that described by older generations.

About the Translators

Orsola Casagrande was a journalist with the daily national Italian paper *il manifesto* for 25 years. She is currently the co-editor of the web magazine *Global Rights*, is fluent in Italian, English, Spanish and Turkish, and reads and speaks Kurdish. Orsola is currently living in Havana. She has reported on the Irish, Kurdish and Basque peace processes, and for the past three years has been covering the Colombia peace negotiations. Her translations into Italian include *The Street* by Gerry Adams (Gamberetti, 1994), *The Second Prison* by Ronan Bennett (Gamberetti, 1995), *The Fountain at the Centre of the World* by Robert Newman,(Giunti,2011). Her own books include: *Minatori: La storia di Tower Colliery* (Miners: The Story of Tower Colliery, Odradek, 2004), *Berxwedan* (Punto Rosso, 2009), and *Europa Domani: Conversazione con Tariq Ramadan* (Jouvence, 2008). The first two of these were also the subjects of documentary films which she wrote and co-directed.

Séamas Carraher is a working class writer and poet who also moonlights as a freelance translator and has also worked as a filmmaker. He is currently supporting long-term homeless street drinkers at night to pay the rent, having been a community activist for over 30 years. Orsola and Séamas have worked together for a number of years translating, writing and publishing in a variety of journals and literary reviews, in both English and Spanish. Orsola and Séamas continue to work together on the web magazine *Global Rights* (www.globalrights. info).